Folk Tales
of Bihar

Nalin Verma is a veteran journalist who has worked in senior editorial positions with *The Telegraph* and *The Statesman*. He began his career a journalist with *The Hindustan Times* in late 80s. He has written extensively on society, politics, and governance of Bihar for over three decades and contributes to several national and international journals as well as digital media platforms regularly. Considered to be the region's one of the most independent journalists, his work is deeply influenced by his time spent with people in the hinterlands. Of late, Nalin has shifted to teaching and research and is a professor at Lovely Professional University at Jalandhar, Punjab.

He is the co-author of the much-acclaimed autobiography of Lalu Prasad Yadav, *Gopalganj to Raisina: My Political Journey*.

Praise for the book

Folk tales constitute a very valuable part of the intangible heritage of India, but are under grave threat as we hurl towards a new definition of 'modernism'. Nalin Verma's highly readable book that retells the folk tales of Bihar is, therefore, a most creditable and relevant attempt to take us back to our roots and retrieve what is in great danger of being lost.

—Pavan Varma, renowned author,
columnist and former diplomat

For its sheer thought and effort, this is a stellar act. In this fast-paced age, Nalin decided to pull the brakes and walk back to see what the past might have to offer our future. What he found was a treasure trove. These are not merely stories, these are gems of our heritage that would have wasted away had Nalin not so passionately and painstakingly shored them up for us and our coming generations.

—Sankarshan Thakur,
Roving Editor of *The Telegraph* and acclaimed author

The Greatest Folk Tales of Bihar

Nalin Verma

RUPA

Published by
Rupa Publications India Pvt. Ltd 2019
7/16, Ansari Road, Daryaganj
New Delhi 110002

Sales centres:
Allahabad Bengaluru Chennai
Hyderabad Jaipur Kathmandu
Kolkata Mumbai

ISBN: 978-93-5333-662-2

Second impression 2020

10 9 8 7 6 5 4 3 2

The moral right of the author has been asserted.

Printed at Repro Knowledge Caste Limited, Mumbai

Contents

Introduction   *vii*

Wisdom of the Birds
1. The Sparrow and Her Crumbs   3
2. The Crow and the Sparrow   7
3. The Village Crow Versus the City Crow   11
4. The Stork and Her New Husband   14
5. The Parrot and His Grandson   17

Animal Kingdom
6. How a Jackal Attained Pundit-hood   23
7. The Boastful Jackal and the Timid Goat   27
8. The Lioness and the Cow   31
9. How the Jackal Got Lessons in Picking Fruits   35
10. The Jackal and the Camel   37
11. The Donkey and the Dog   40
12. How the Jackal Preyed on the Goat   42

Survival in the Wild
13. The Poor Brahmin and His Seven Daughters   47
14. The Fear of Tiptipwa   51
15. The Cobbler and the Washerman   55

Folk Fun

16. The Gossiper   63
17. The Simpleton   66
18. Munshiji and Raiji   70

Gods, Demons and Faith

19. The Priest and the Thugs   75
20. The Young Boy and Hanumanji   80
21. The Skull and Raghobaba   83
22. The Rakshasi's Sacrifice   86
23. The Elephant and the Worms   89
24. The Brahmin and the Washerwoman   92

Pranks, Intrigues, Struggle and Entertainment

25. The Scholar and His 'Heavenly' Beard   99
26. The Malpua Tale   102
27. Andher Nagari, Chowpat Raja
    (The Dark City and the Whimsical King)   106
28. The Sinner and the Khaini   110
29. The Leaf and the Lump   112
30. Ulua, Bulua and I   114
31. The Badshah and His Youngest Daughter   115
32. The Shyamkaran Horse   119
33. The Mahout and the Dogs   125
34. Bharbitan   127

Bhikhari Thakur's Popular Folklores

35. Gabarghichor   135
36. The Daughter's Suffering   140

The Lore of Love

37. Saranga and Sadabrij   151

Epilogue: How These Tales Were Collected   165
Acknowledgements   181
Glossary   183

Introduction

'Ae Ahiya tu mahiya chaata, chala chali Kaluhari mein.
Ahiya ke pahiya phaans gaeel baat-e Bangal ke khadi mein.
Tohra maja aayee Subedar bhai sang mahiya chaat-e
mein.'

How much of history can the spoken words preserve? How much of the past can be captured in verse? Whenever these questions pop up, the lines I had heard in my village in Bihar's Siwan district as a teenager, and which I have mentioned above, come to mind.

The lines mock Yahya Khan, Pakistan's then president and army chief who presided over the country at the time of its defeat from India in the 1971 war that created Bangladesh.

Diljar Mian, a fellow Muslim in my village, would parrot these lines in the sing-song way typical of rural Bihar. Roughly translated, they mean: 'O Yahya Khan, come lick *mahiya* with us/Let us go together to *kaluhari*/Yahya's wheels are stuck in the Bay of Bengal/He will have fun licking mahiya with brother Subedar.'

Diljar Mian came from a poor barber-farmer family. His older brother, Subedar Mian, swept Dhaka's streets for a living, one of the many migrant workers from villages in Bihar before the Partition. Subedar would send money to his family and visit them once a year. But neither Diljar nor other villagers like him with kin in the erstwhile East Pakistan had seen or heard about their loved ones after India was partitioned in 1947.

My fellow villagers hardly bothered about the Partition; but they missed Subedar, who they had not seen for 23 years.

I was born 13 years after the Partition, but I had heard stories about Subedar, stories that grew more fantastic with each year passing without a word of his whereabouts. He had been a chowkidar who would patrol in the dark with a spear on his shoulder, sporting a peacock-feathered headgear that struck fear in the hearts of dacoits and thugs eyeing our village. He had been the *chacha* who had taught the kids how to wrestle.

Pakistan's defeat and the creation of Bangladesh with India's help had rekindled hope among the villagers and they believed that they would be able to see Subedar again. '*Ae Ahiya tu mahiya chaata...*' was a reflection of their collective anger towards Khan—metaphor for Pakistan—who had held their Subedar back. They wished Khan would be vanquished and dragged off his high horse, down to their level, so that they could poke fun at him. The rhyme mocks Khan and celebrates the general's fall to ordinariness. As the middle-aged Diljar would sing away, the villagers would laugh their guts out. It was a poem that connected their lives to the echoes of the war.

The sugar cane the villagers grew was used to make *mitha*. The sugar cane was juiced using a contraption that a bullock drove round and round in a circle. The juice obtained was then filtered using a piece of cotton cloth as a sieve into large pitchers that were emptied into a *kadahi*—eight feet in diameter—placed on a *bhatthi*. It took seven to eight hours of boiling on a low but consistent flame to turn the juice into loose sticky dough that was left to cool down and solidify into mitha. As the cane juice boiled, it oozed foam and bubbles that the farmers skimmed out and served on banyan or banana leaves. It was called mahiya. The villagers loved licking mahiya. They would gossip, crack jokes and poke fun at others over mahiya—the labour of their love.

I don't know if Diljar had crafted the Yahya song himself or had heard it somewhere else. But it didn't matter much. Like Diljar, many other villagers were natural bards. Composing verses, telling stories and singing ballads came naturally to them. They enjoyed and sang the verses rather than bothering about the source of their composition. Though mostly illiterate, they had their own chisels to shape their lyrics. They always found the right words; had the elephantine memory needed to remember the numerous stories and songs passed down the generations along with the knack to reproduce them to the amusement of all.

Diljar's song was in Bhojpuri, a dialect of the Hindi language. It sang of what the villagers longed to hear. That's why the song struck a chord with the listeners, sending them into raptures. I remember gusty renditions of it later by a band of folk singers to the accompaniment of dholak, *jhal* and *majira*. Not all folk songs had so contemporary a theme, though. Usually, the village folklorists chose local characters, animals, birds, Gods and Goddesses as subjects of their rhymes and rhythms. They took the shape of satire, drama, novellas and ballads.

~

The stories I had heard in my village, Daraili Mathia, were

popular across the state and in large parts of the Bhojpuri-speaking belt of Uttar Pradesh. In fact, these stories, encapsulating the local culture and universal messages, travelled to Pakistan and Bangladesh, which had a large number of migrant workers from the region, settled there in the wake of Partition. The folk tales also travelled to Mauritius, Jamaica, Trinidad and the Caribbean, which had Bhojpuri speakers migrating in hordes as indentured labourers during the nineteenth and the twentieth centuries.

Daraili Mathia is tucked away in a corner of the Siwan district in the eastern Indian state of Bihar. I was born and brought up, and learnt to walk and talk on its dusty and often mud-filled streets, snaking through a maze of sugar cane, mustard, wheat and paddy fields. It is about 150 kilometres northwest of Patna, Bihar's capital, where I cut my professional teeth as a journalist.

I wonder if the stories I had heard in my village during my childhood and which I have reproduced in this book will help the next generations learn about the culture their forefathers spread to different parts of the globe.

Most villagers were poor and backward-caste cultivators, for whom education meant nothing. There were also six Kayastha families—a caste group known for its educational prowess. But the Kayasthas of my village were not much educated. Some of them, who could just about read and write, wanted their children to leave the village as early as possible to land jobs only education could get them. I was one of them.

Though working and residing in an urban centre, I keep visiting my village to refresh my memories of that life, to make sure they did not vanish from the tendrils of my consciousness. In this book, I have recounted what I heard from my mother, father and grandfather, as well as other villagers during my wonder years. The stories are raw because I have retold them just the way I had heard them. If they resonate with you, it will be because of the innate quality of the stories and the craft of the original bards. And if you find them off-putting, that would entirely be because of my inadequacy as a storyteller.

❧

My village was like many other villages in Bihar at that time—a self-contained world with no motorable road to link it to the outside world. You had to walk at least five kilometres through zigzag pathways, squeezing past prickly brambles to get to Kanhauli to board the lone bus that ferried the village folks to Darauli-Mairwa-Siwan and back. Only the elders who had legal cases to fight in the courts of Siwan or buy clothes for their family members for festivals and weddings would take the bus ride. Should an exigency arise, my father would get up and start walking much before dawn to catch the solitary bus.

I had not seen a bus by the time I had heard most of these stories. I had travelled in bullock carts, and was still learning to ride the bicycle my father had bought for me. There was no electricity in the village. Diyas lit homes after sunset. I was privileged to have a hurricane lantern my father had brought from the nearest town, Siwan, to help me read after dark. My father had a handheld torch, but he rarely switched it on except when he went out to answer nature's call in the open at night. If the batteries would get discharged, he would need money, time and energy to fetch them from Siwan. This is why he feared the discharge of the batteries and therefore always kept the torch beyond the reach of children.

The telephone was an unusual thing then, but we would occasionally see a *hawai jahaj* flitting across the azure sky over our heads. We would giggle and mischievously throw stones at it as if to bring it down. We would ask the elders what those flying objects were, but would never get a clear answer.

The howls of jackals coming from the sugar cane fields on the borders of the village after sunset would strike fear in the hearts of children. We would play with pets while listening to the sweet music of birds—nightingales, parrots, sparrows and pigeons—chirping on the trees around us. I knew the difference between the tweets of a sparrow and a pigeon before I had ever heard a car horn, never mind Twitter.

❧

Coming back to the rhyme, Yahya Khan became a household name in this village, thanks to a box that talked. It spoke of how the Indian Army chief, General Manekshaw, had whipped Pakistan President Yahya Khan's back. It was a radio a fellow villager Gopal had got as dowry.

Villagers religiously flocked to Gopal's home to listen with rapt attention to the *Akashwani*'s morning and evening news bulletins for updates on the war, believing that Manekshaw beating Khan was the only way to get back their Subedar. Manekshaw had emerged as their hero. They would cheer the newsreader as he spoke of how the Indian Army was marching to victory. When one day it was announced that India had defeated Pakistan, they cheered Manekshaw and jeered at Khan, '*Ae Ahiya tu mahia chata...*', and broke into singing in unison.

Gopal's father, Lakhi Sahu, was an unfriendly sort. He loathed fun. Even a fleeting look at him could make someone regret cracking a joke. He was at his mellowest in the company of his cattle. But it was his house that had the radio. So the villagers would cajole him into letting them listen to the news bulletins. Lakhi's contemporaries knew that he, too, missed

Subedar, with whom he had played in the village streets. When Diljar would sing, '*Ae Ahiya tu mahia chaata*', Lakhi would guffaw. I had been genuinely surprised that Lakhi could laugh.

Soon, the song became an even bigger 'hit'. The villagers strung the words up in a Holi tune, and sang it collectively with a battery of percussion—dholak, jhal, *pakwaj* and majira—and a flute, played by the village elder Madhav chacha, backed them up.

Around the same time, an older folk song was slipping off the village charts, so to speak. It went like this:

'*Arjun ke avtaar Hitler duniya ke hilaule baa*
Roosh ke jitlas France ke jitlas England niyaraule baa
mauga Gandhi chhod ke Bose ke dost banwale baa.'

It extolled Hitler and belittled Gandhi. Roughly translated, it means: 'An incarnation of Arjuna, Hitler has shaken the world. He has conquered Russia, France and is closing in on England. Shunning effeminate Gandhi he has befriended Subhas Chandra Bose.'

Basudeo Lal, an elderly farmer, would sing this one occasionally at the evening *chowpal*. Some other elders would accompany him on the dholak and jhal groove, while youngsters would join in the singing.

The song was rooted in World War II. The world war coincided with Gandhi's leading the peaceful movement of non-cooperation against the British colonists. Gandhi, of course, became the Mahatma after he chose Bihar's Champaran region—barely 60 kilometres from my village Daraili Mathia—to launch his struggle against the British. My village elders recalled how Gandhi Baba had travelled to them preaching truth and non-violence in the battle against *ghulami*.

It was during the dog days of World War II that the

revolutionary from Bengal, Bose, formed an army, the Azad Hind Fauj, and joined hands with Hitler to drive the Brits out of India. Unlike Gandhi, Bose had hardly travelled to our area. The people hadn't seen him. As for Hitler, he could have been from the moon for the villagers.

Still, the führer became a part of the Bihari song, where he was equated even with Arjuna—a hero in India's greatest epic, the *Mahabharata*. The song hailed Hitler because he had befriended Bose, who 'at least' tried to kick the Brits' butts, and shunned the 'namby-pamby' Gandhi, who had not proved to be a Mahatma by then.

Gandhi, I knew. The currency notes printed after Independence bore his mugshot. My father's elder brother D.C. Verma was a freedom fighter who had been jailed for years for participating in the freedom struggle that Gandhi led. My villagers had seen Gandhi. Gandhi was also a topic in our primary-school textbooks. But the first time I came to know of Hitler was because of this particular folk song. The villagers—even Basudeo chacha—did not know about Hitler or World War II beyond this song. It was hard to figure out how Hitler and Bose caught the folklorists' imaginations.

I'm not sure whether this folk lyric had been composed by my villagers or it had travelled to their tongues from elsewhere. What I can guess is that there was always something at different stages of oral history to connect the villagers with national and international events. If anything, the song on Hitler, Gandhi and Bose brings to the fore that there were sections of people who idolized Hitler and Bose for their 'bravery' against the British and reserved contempt for Gandhi and his peaceful ways that they interpreted as 'meek surrender' to the guns of the British rulers.

Another person who had fuelled curiosity among the

villagers was young Lalu Prasad Yadav. Lalu belonged to Phulwaria village in the neighbouring Gopalganj district— barely 30 kilometres from Daraili Mathia. The radio blared news about Lalu's emergence as a big student leader at Patna University. The villagers talked about how Lalu, a local boy, had become a disciple of the great freedom fighter, Jayaprakash Narayan, and how he was bravely fighting for the cause of the people under JP's stewardship. Lalu had a bond with the villagers for he belonged to them. But Lalu then was just a subject of occasional and passing discussion among the villagers.

The enemy's enemy is a friend—perhaps that explains the folklorists' love for Hitler over Gandhi. The song also indicates that despite their isolation, the villagers felt the heat of the British rule and picked up Hitler to cheer against the British— their enemy's enemy.

But, by the time Yahya came in the scene, this song was fading like the memories of the Raj. Basudeo chacha was the last person who would occasionally sing it. And when he could sing it no more, the song died.

❦

The two verses, which expressed the events separated by decades, were just the tip of the colossal iceberg of oral history. The folklorists primarily derived their themes from the universal realities of life—social relationships, family values, changing seasons, harvest, flowers, or changes of any kind.

The festival of Holi celebrated the end of dreary autumn and the arrival of the colourful *basant*, which brought along an array of rabi crops like wheat, barley, gram, sugar cane, mustard and peas growing in green fields, extending up to the distant horizon. Many songs popular among the villagers likened the earth covered with yellow mustard flowers swaying in the cool breeze to a young woman in a captivating dress. Holi fuelled eroticism, which was reflected in the songs of this festival, depicting the spicy relationship between *devar* and *bhabhi*. The singers used the dalliance between playful Lord Krishna and his aunt-lover Radha to add romance to their folklores.

Chaita songs followed Holi. They spoke of the pain of separation of newly-wed couples. The husbands worked in faraway cities to earn their livelihood. Calcutta (now Kolkata) figured prominently in the songs of my village because many worked there. The chaita songs described how the young wives craved their husbands' early return with clothes and jewellery for them. Pigeons served as messengers between the wife and the husband, separated by long distances. The caw of a crow on the terrace was taken to be a signal for the arrival of a dear one whereas the tweeting of sparrows indicated the happiness of Laxmi—the Goddess of wealth. When a crow pecked a person's head, it meant death was coming, and if a vulture sat atop a home, it spelled disaster for its occupants.

The epics, *Ramayana* and *Mahabharata*, and their characters, Krishna, Radha, Rama, Sita and several other Gods and Goddesses played a role in the folk songs. So did animals and birds. The folklorists sang to celebrate special occasions like the birth of a child or marriage.

The villagers crooned, danced and enacted dramas to take a break from the monotony *of everyday life.* These folk activities formed and strengthened social bonding.

The daily business of living was a struggle for the villagers. They would toil hard to manage two square meals for the family. A complete meal of rice, dal, vegetables and curd was a luxury a peasant or a cultivator could hardly afford. Whether it was the scorching heat of midsummer days, the biting cold of winter or the long spells of monsoon rain, daily toil was their lot. They sat huddled around *kaud* to ward off the winter chill as they had no blankets and blazers to cover themselves with.

The aim of this book is to retell the folk tales—a segment of the diverse oral tradition—that I have heard and grown up with. I have tried to keep out what I have learnt from the books. I have retold here what I gathered in oral form from the villagers, most of them unlettered.

Some tales are full of ballads. For example, the love story of Saranga and Sadabrij. A village folklorist, Patru Ahir, specialized in narrating and singing Saranga-Sadabrij's love saga. When he sang it in his mellifluous voice, it drew the village youths to him like a magnet. It was much later in life that I read about the Pied Piper who had hordes of rats following him as he played on his flute. Looking back, I remember being one of the youngsters in a similar herd rushing to listen to Saranga-Sadabrij's romantic escapades. I have tried to simplify the ballads in order to make them intelligible to the readers. I may not have succeeded in recreating the exact slang and circumstances in the ballads through the medium of the written word in this book, but I have attempted to retain their essence.

This book has two dramas—*Gabarghichor* and *Beti bechwa*—authored and played by Bhikhari Thakur, a master folklorist whose fame travelled far beyond the borders of Bihar. Scholars of Hindi literature have described him as the 'Shakespeare of Bhojpuri'. Born into a poor barber family of Kutubpur in the Saran district of north Bihar, barely 60 kilometres from my village, Bhikhari dominated the folk scene for decades in the twentieth century. His songs and dramas highlighted social disparity, caste divide, the prevalence of child marriage and other ills afflicting society. The Bihar Rashtrabhasa Parishad—a body set up to preserve native languages—has documented Bhikhari's creations in a book, *Bhikhari Thakur Rachnavali*. I have retold only *Gabarghichor* and *Beti bechwa* because I had watched Bhikhari Thakur's team enacting these stories on the streets of my village. Bhikhari Thakur was dead by then.

I cannot claim to be the first to retell these folk tales in the form of oral tradition. In fact, the great Indian classics, the *Ramayana* and *Mahabharata*, are also believed to have existed as popular narratives for centuries before Valmiki and Ved Vyas turned them into written words.

Panchatantra—believed to be a 2,000-year-old collection of fables, imparting lessons in wisdom, morality and statecraft to three princes—is still popular amongst the young and the old alike across continents. Through the stories, Vishnusarman—the saint and author of the *Panchatantra*—provides guidelines to the princes on what is right and what is wrong in a given situation.

Panchatantra has been translated in over fifty languages. This highlights its longevity and acceptability across the linguistic divisions of the world. I read the latest version of *Panchatantra* authored by Kenneth Anderson alias Krishna Dharma, a British scholar, who has translated other Indian scriptures too. His is probably the latest version in English published by Torchlight Publishing (USA) in 2004.

I have tried to leave out the tales that have appeared in *Panchatantra* and *Jataka* stories (related to the birth of Gautam Buddha) and other possible treatises of folk tales. As I come from a village in Bihar—the state with a vast reservoir of tales and fables since time immemorial—I have taken care to read as many recorded folk tales as I could lay my hands on. That makes it clear that I do not claim to be the sole recorder of these tales.

I have retold what I have experienced. I have visited my village several times to rebuild the stories and reimagine the situations. But the stories are original. I have given credit to their narrators. But even they are not the creators of the stories. They just retold what they had heard from their peers or predecessors.

I encountered many people in different parts of Bihar retelling these stories when I grew up and travelled among them. Over the years, I came to realize that the stories were common to almost all the villages in Bihar, transcending a plethora of dialects—Bhojpuri, Maithili, Magahi, Angika and Vajjika—spoken in the five linguistic divisions of the state.

I can't determine the exact age of these stories. They might have taken shape over several centuries, from the Mauryan times to the British period. Mine is not a scholarly work. It is just a reproduction of what I had heard while growing up in situations that have drastically changed over the decades.

These stories may be lost to the fast-changing times. The kind of kaluhari mentioned earlier is not seen today, and bullocks no longer run them. The farmers crush sugar cane in machine-driven rollers. The interactive chowpal that once drew folklorists and their audience have vanished too.

Concrete roads have replaced the zigzag uneven and unpaved *pagdandis* negotiating which was always a challenge as it required extra care and effort to avoid losing balance and tumbling down. The villagers no longer travel in bullock carts due to the advent of all sorts of vehicles—cars, jeeps and motorcycles. The once ubiquitous radio is passé and has been replaced by TVs and smartphones. Gone are the days of village chowpals and community gatherings. In their free time, people remain either glued to the 'idiot box' or are busy fiddling with their mobile phones. Folklores are dying, and so are their singers. Patru, Diljar and Basudeo had learnt the lore from their forefathers, who, in turn, had inherited them from their forefathers. But the age-old tradition seems to have stopped at the three above mentioned stalwarts who had no enthusiastic disciples to whom they could pass on the mantle.

This book doesn't attempt a critique of the process of change; it is just an effort at preserving the vignettes that sustained village life for centuries before the winds of change began to blow. The preservation of cultural icons cast in stones like the Taj Mahal, Ashokan Pillars and Egyptian Pyramids calls for an exploration of whether the folk tales—the monuments of villagers' imagination—can also be preserved. This book in your hands attempts to do exactly that.

I happened to accompany Bill Gates—the founder of Microsoft who criss-crosses the continents on his private jet— on a boat journey across River Kosi on the way to Gularia, a small village in Bihar's Khagaria district, on 12 June 2010. As the boat reached midstream, it started swerving from one side to the other and back while sailing against the strong currents of the swollen river, causing panic among those on board. With every swerve of the boat, the situation became scarier. To lessen the fears of the unnerved passengers, the boatman broke into a prayer song that sought to propitiate the river god. To our surprise, the incantation of the hymn had a soothing effect on the nerves of the scared passengers. An amused Bill then asked me to explain the situation.

I have no idea whether Bill Gates still remembers the journey but I keep wondering what about the boatman's song had calmed the passengers' jittery nerves in the turbulent streams. Perhaps, the simple folks had faith that the boatman's prayer would calm the rage of Mother Kosi, and their nervousness was gone.

Bill Gates enjoyed the situation. We reached the riverbank safe and happy. Suddenly, this thought crossed my mind: Why can't the users of Bill's Microsoft and the folklores sail together? I'm afraid many people might find the idea rather outlandish. But this book is a humble attempt at preserving the monument of creativity that is in its death throes.

The first story that I learnt in school was '*Kawwa aur Ghara*' (The Crow and the Pitcher), prescribed in the Hindi textbook for our primary classes at Basic School, Daraili Mathia—my alma mater. Our teacher, Phuleshwar Pandey, had told us this story. It was a tradition to revere our teacher and refer to him as 'Master Sahib'. Addressing a teacher by name amounted to irreverence and 'sir' was not yet known among the village students.

The story went like this:

> There was a crow. On a hot summer day, he felt extremely thirsty. He flew from one place to another in search of water. He was dejected to find that all the ponds had dried up. In the course of the search, his eyes fell upon a pitcher placed near a well. He flew down and sat on the edge of the pitcher and peeped in, only to discover a little water left at the bottom of the pitcher. His beak couldn't have reached that level. He saw some pebbles scattered around and had a brainwave. He picked up the pebbles and dropped them in the pitcher one after another. The level of water rose and the crow was able to quench his thirst.

At the end of the story, Master Sahib enlightened us with the lesson it conveyed: 'The story teaches us to be wise and ingenious in a challenging situation, like the crow that turned an adverse situation to its advantage, acting with wisdom to quench its thirst.'

I had heard the story before Master Sahib taught it in the classroom. My grandmother, Sona Devi, had narrated it to me much before I had stepped in the school. But Master Sahib imparted knowledge through the written words of the textbook. It was him who acquainted me with letters.

I recently met Muskan and Afsana, great-grandkids of Diljar Mian, and Ankit and Rahul, the grandchildren of Diljar's contemporaries. Muskan, Afsana, Ankit and Rahul are all primary-class students at the same school. The children, too, had the 'Crow-Pitcher' story in their textbook. But they didn't know that their grandparents and great-grandparents had countless such stories to tell them as well.

I wish this book informs Muskan, Afsana, Ankit and Rahul about the mastery their forefathers had in telling stories. The building of the school had collapsed by the time I went there to take initial lessons in letters and numbers. We sat on the debris of the fallen building, beneath a large peepul tree there. Then, the school just had a few children.

The Basic School, Daraili Mathia, has a good building today. Almost all the children in the village go to the school, which now has teachers who dress in trousers and T-shirt unlike our Master Sahib who wore dhoti and kurta.

The first poem that I had memorized from the textbook was: '*Peepul ke patte gol-gol, kuchh kahte-rahte dol-dol*' (The peepul's leaves are all round, they seem to keep shaking and telling us something). Our verbal recital of the poem resonated with the peepul leaves fluttering in the wind above our heads.

The poem still exists in some Hindi textbooks. But the peepul tree located in the school disappeared from the scene a long time ago.

Wisdom of the Birds

The Sparrow and Her Crumbs

L ong ago, there lived a sparrow. Once, she picked up a grain of gram and carried it to a stone grinder to break it into two bits. In the process of grinding, a part of the grain came out while the rest of it remained stuck in the wooden pricket that worked as the grinder's pivot.

The sparrow repeatedly pecked into the pricket, trying to extricate the trapped morsel, but failed. Exhausted, she rushed to a woodcutter and pleaded, 'O woodcutter! Rip the pricket. My crumb is in the pricket. What shall I eat and what shall I carry for my journey overseas?'

The woodcutter, agitated at the bird's request, retorted, 'Get lost! Am I a fool that I will rip the whole pricket for a piece of grain?'

The sparrow, too, lost her temper. She approached the king and pleaded, 'O king! Punish the woodcutter. The woodcutter wouldn't rip the pricket. My crumb is in the pricket. What shall I eat and what shall I carry for my journey overseas?'

The king rejected the sparrow's plea, arguing that it was unjust to punish the woodcutter for a morsel of grain. Fluttering and chirping, the sparrow went to the queen and entreated, 'O queen! Counsel the king. The king wouldn't punish the woodcutter. The woodcutter wouldn't rip the pricket. My crumb is in the pricket. What shall I eat and what shall I carry for my journey overseas?'

The queen, too, refused to entertain the sparrow's request, 'I can't counsel the king for such a small thing.'

The sparrow then went to a snake and pleaded, 'O snake! Bite the queen. The queen wouldn't counsel the king. The king wouldn't punish the woodcutter. The woodcutter wouldn't rip the pricket. My crumb is in the pricket. What shall I eat and what shall I carry for my journey overseas?'

'Are you insane? How can I bite the queen for a morsel of grain?' hissed the snake, turning down the sparrow's plea.

Disappointed, the sparrow went to a stick and begged, 'O stick! Kill the snake. The snake wouldn't bite the queen. The queen wouldn't counsel the king. The king wouldn't punish the woodcutter. The woodcutter wouldn't rip the pricket. My crumb is in the pricket. What shall I eat and what shall I carry for my journey overseas?'

The stick, too, refused to help the sparrow. Not willing to give up hope, she shouted out to the fire, 'O fire! Burn the stick. The stick wouldn't kill the snake. The snake wouldn't bite the queen. The queen wouldn't counsel the king. The king wouldn't punish the woodcutter. The woodcutter wouldn't rip the pricket. My crumb is in the pricket. What shall I eat and what shall I carry for my journey overseas?'

'Get out. I will not burn the stick for a morsel of grain,' shouted back the fire.

The sparrow approached the ocean, 'O ocean! Extinguish the fire. The fire wouldn't burn the stick. The stick wouldn't kill the snake. The snake wouldn't bite the queen. The queen wouldn't counsel the king. The king wouldn't punish the woodcutter. The woodcutter wouldn't rip the pricket. My crumb is in the pricket. What shall I eat and what shall I carry for my journey overseas?'

As the ocean snubbed the sparrow, she flew to an elephant. 'O elephant! Please swallow the ocean. The ocean wouldn't extinguish the fire. The fire would not burn the stick. The stick wouldn't kill the snake. The snake wouldn't bite the queen. The queen would not counsel the king. The king wouldn't punish the woodcutter. The woodcutter wouldn't rip the pricket. My crumb is in the pricket. What shall I eat and what shall I carry for my journey overseas?'

Already thirsty, the elephant thought it could achieve two goals if it fulfilled the sparrow's wish. Its thirst would be quenched and the sparrow would be obliged. So, the elephant headed towards the ocean with the sparrow in tow.

The ocean was scared to see the elephant approach it menacingly. The ocean implored, 'Do not swallow me, please. I will extinguish the fire.'

The ocean went to the fire. The fire got nervous and pleaded, 'Do not extinguish me, please. I will burn the stick.'

As the fire leapt to burn the stick, the stick begged for mercy, 'Do not burn me, please. I will kill the snake.'

When the stick went to kill the snake, the snake pleaded, 'Have mercy on me, please. I will bite the queen.'

As the snake crawled to dig its fangs into the queen, the queen said, 'Spare my life, please. I will counsel the king.'

When the queen went to counsel the king, he said, 'Cheer up, dear. I will punish the woodcutter.'

As the king called the woodcutter to punish him, the woodcutter said, 'Do not punish me, please. I will rip the pricket.'

When the woodcutter went to rip the pricket, the pricket

pleaded, 'No one should rip me apart. I am splitting on my own.'

The pricket split, throwing the crumb out. The sparrow picked up the crumb and flew off merrily.

Be positive and never give up—success will come to you.

THE GREATEST FOLK TALES OF BIHAR

The Crow and the Sparrow

Once, there lived a crow named Banati. He was wicked and cruel. He loved to torment the weaker birds. One day, the crow caught hold of a little sparrow and prepared to eat her up. The blood-curdling prospect of certain death sent a shiver down the spine of the poor sparrow.

But the bird was wise and religious, with deep faith in Gods and Goddesses. She thought of using her wisdom and her faith in the divine powers of Mother Ganga—the holy river—to ward off the danger.

She beseeched the crow, 'I won't stop you from eating me. But I would like you to abide by some rules and rituals before that. You should sanctify your beak with the water of Mother Ganga first. My meat will taste better if you eat it with your sanctified beak.'

'I already have the sparrow in my control. She will only taste better if I accept her advice,' Banati thought, finding merit in the sparrow's words. He entangled her in his nest and flew off to sanctify his beak in the river.

Relieved, the sparrow began praying fervently to Mother Ganga. 'O Mother! If you save me, I will offer you three grains

7

of rice and a drop of curd,' she vowed.

The ill-mannered crow reached the river and shouted pejoratively, 'Ganglo, Ganglo, Ganglo!'

Ignoring his foul manners, Ganga asked calmly, 'What have you come for, Banati?'

The crow said mischievously, 'I am in a great hurry. Let me dip my beak in your sacred water to purify it before eating the sparrow—delicious and yummy!'

Politely, the river reasoned, 'Do you know that lakhs of people take holy dips in me every day? By dipping your beak, you will make the entire river impure. Many people draw my water for ablutions and to purify offerings for Gods and Goddesses. You better go to a potter and ask for an earthen bowl. I will pour water into the bowl so that you can purify your beak and eat the sparrow.'

The crow approached the potter, shouting loudly, 'Potter, potter, potter!'

The potter ignored the crow's impish conduct and said, 'You are a guest. Tell me, what can I do for you?'

The crow said, 'Give me a bowl. Ganga will pour her water into it so that I can dip my beak. Then I will eat the sparrow—delicious and yummy.'

The potter said, 'I don't have clay as of now. Bring me a deer's antler; I will use it to dig the earth and make a bowl for you.'

The crow went to the deer and yelled, 'Deer, deer, deer! Give me your horn so that the potter can dig the soil. The potter will use it to make the bowl. Ganga will pour her water into it. I will dip my beak into the water, and eat the sparrow—delicious and yummy.'

The deer shot back, 'How can I break my antler by myself? Your beak is too weak to break it. I suggest you ask a dog to break a portion of my antler. I will then readily give it to you.'

The crow went to a dog and shouted, 'Dingo, Dingo, Dingo! Break the deer's antler. The potter will dig the earth and make a bowl with it. Ganga will pour her water into it. I will dip my beak into the water, and then, I will eat the sparrow—delicious and yummy.'

The dog barked, 'I haven't eaten anything for long and I am hungry. Bring me some milk. I will drink milk to gain my strength. Then, I will break the deer's antler.'

Banati went to a cow and shouted, 'Cow, cow, cow! Give me milk. The dog will drink it. He will break the deer's antler. The potter will then dig the earth and make a bowl with it. Ganga will pour her water into it. I will then dip my beak in the water and eat the sparrow—delicious and yummy.'

The cow said, 'My calf has emptied my udders. Bring me some grass. I will have enough milk to give after I eat the green grass.'

The crow approached the gardener and shouted, 'Gardener, gardener, gardener! Give me grass for the cow to eat. She will give me milk. The dog will drink it. He will then break the deer's antler. The potter will be able to dig the earth with it and make a bowl. Ganga will pour her water into it. I will then dip my beak in the water and eat the sparrow—delicious and yummy.'

The gardener said, 'I don't have a sickle right now. Go to the blacksmith and bring a sickle so that I can cut the grass for you.'

The crow went to the blacksmith and shouted, 'Blacksmith, blacksmith, blacksmith! Give me a sickle. The gardener will cut the grass. The cow will eat it and give me milk. The dog will drink it. He will break the deer's antler. The potter will dig the earth to make a bowl. Ganga will pour her water into

9

it. I will then dip my beak in the water and eat the sparrow—delicious and yummy.'

The blacksmith was already upset for he had spent long hours melting iron and making tools. 'This crow wants to make me a participant in his sin. The innocent sparrow has done no wrong to me. Why should I help Banati in perpetrating cruelty on a small bird? 'the blacksmith wondered and decided to end Banati's pranks once and for all.

The blacksmith asked, 'Which colour would you like—black or red?'The crow, black himself, did not like his colour. The idea of getting a red-coloured sickle fascinated him and he asked for it.

The blacksmith put the iron into the fire to melt and mould it into a sickle. He brought the sickle out when it was red-hot, signalling the crow to take it in his beak. Desperate to eat the sparrow, the crow hurriedly tried to hold the red-hot sickle in his beak and died instantly. He could not even utter a single 'caw-caw'.

The news of Banati's death spread fast in the forest. Soon, other birds gathered to untangle the little sparrow that lived merrily thereafter.

Be wise, industrious and faithful.

The Village Crow Versus the City Crow

A crow happily lived in a certain village. The village fields were full of wheat, paddy, chickpeas and millets—enough for the crow to eat and live merrily.

Once, the village was struck with famine. The crops died and the ponds dried up. There was an enormous shortage of grains and water, making lives miserable for people, animals and birds. The residents began migrating elsewhere in search of food and livelihood.

The crow was sad to see the barren fields and dried-up waterbodies. His belly hurt with the pinch of hunger. Starved and enervated, the crow, too, decided to migrate to a city in search of food and water.

He flew to the outskirts of a city and sat on a banyan tree. As it happened, another crow, which was a city dweller, joined the village crow sitting on the branch.

The sight of a peer thrilled the village crow, who said, 'I feel lucky for I have gotten a friend from the city. I am sure you will guide me and help me find something to eat and drink.'

The city crow reacted quite unexpectedly. 'You will have

11

to be wise to live in the city. There is no scope for fools here. You have lived in the village throughout your life. Obviously, you are a fool devoid of the skill and smartness needed to survive in the city.'

The village crow politely said, 'God has imparted us better wisdom in comparison to other birds. I don't think I am a fool and incapable of living and earning my livelihood in the city. As a fellow from the same race I expect you to guide me to the places where I can pick up food to eat and water to drink.'

The city crow retorted, 'Impossible! There are neither crop-filled farms nor water-filled ponds available freely in the city. Policemen holding canes guard all the crops and sources of water here. One small mistake can cost you your life. Also, compared to the kind-hearted villagers who attach some sort of divinity to birds, the city dwellers are ruthless. They will kill you without thinking twice.'

Arguing about wisdom and cleverness for a while, the village crow and the city crow got locked in a heated squabble over who was wiser. In the meantime, the city crow saw a young boy holding a jalebi and walking lazily on the street near the tree. The city crow proposed, 'We should both try to snatch the jalebi from the boy in turns. The one who succeeds in snatching the jalebi from the boy will be considered wiser.'

The village crow agreed, asking his peer from the city to make the first attempt. The city crow flew off to snatch the jalebi from the boy. But as the boy saw the crow hovering over his head, he put the sweetmeat in his mouth and locked his lips.

Disappointed, the city crow returned to the tree. Now it was the village crow's turn. The village crow swooped down on the boy, knocking his beak on his head. The boy cried and ended up dropping the jalebi from his mouth, which the crow picked up and flew off to the tree.

The city crow was ashamed of his defeat at the hands of the village crow. 'You are more tactical than me when it comes to operating in the city. My good wishes are with you,' the city crow said.

One should never underestimate anyone.

The Stork and Her New Husband

A stork left her in-laws' home in a fit of anger and was fleeing when she saw a banyan tree with its lush green branches on the way. The tree noticed the stork hurrying past dejectedly and inquired, 'Why are you looking so upset? Where are you going?'

The stork said, 'I am deeply hurt as my mother-in-law scolded me for no genuine reason. I am on my way to my parents' home.'

The tree asked kindly, 'Why did your mother-in-law scold you? You are so comely and lovable.'

The stork said, 'I ate a morsel of grain while sifting rice grains from the husk and that infuriated her. She screamed at me and I yelled back. We got entangled in this vicious brawl which culminated in my decision to leave her in a huff and head for my parents' home.'

The tree, captivated by the beauty of the bird, offered her his companionship. 'Will you live with me?' he asked, his rustling leaves sounding like water cascading from a fall.

The stork enquired, 'What will you offer me to eat and drink, and where will I sleep?'

The tree said, 'I will offer you my sweet fruits to eat and my soft leaves to sleep on.'

But the stork was not impressed. 'You are a stationary entity, standing lazily in one place. You can't take me on rounds. I will get bored in your company,' she said and walked past the tree.

On her way ahead, she saw a stoutly-built bull, which, too, fell for her beauty. The bull enquired about the reason for the stork's glumness and the bird repeated the same thing to him. Struck as he was with the bird's beauty, the bull entreated, 'O beautiful maiden! It will be my pleasure if you agree to live with me.'

The bird asked, 'What you will offer me to eat, drink and sleep on?'

The bull promptly replied, 'I will feed you fresh vegetables and green grass. I will take you on my hump to the places you like. I will offer you my soft back to sleep on.'

'But you are too huge and unwieldy. If you accidentally keep one of your hoofs or horns on me I will die instantly. It is too risky to live with you,' the stork said and walked past him.

As she moved on, she saw a male stork standing on a pond's edge, looking for fish in the water. The male stork was a widower; his wife had passed away sometime back. The male stork, too, was looking for a suitable partner when the female stork passed by.

Finding the female stork a godsend, the male stork offered her a conjugal life. The female stork found the male bird's offer suitable. She asked what he would feed and offer her to sleep on.

The male stork promptly said, 'I will offer you delicious fish to eat. I will love you and keep you close to my heart, guarding you with my feathers against rain and shine.'

The female stork agreed to begin a new life with her newly-found partner.

One day, the male stork caught plenty of fish, and holding them in his beak, he brought them to his wife. The female stork was an excellent cook. She lit the oven and put the fish in a pan to cook. She headed towards the pond to fetch water while warning her husband, 'Don't touch the fish till I come back. The pan is hot as the fish are being cooked. If you touch them you will get burnt.'

But the aroma wafting from the pan stoked the stork's desire to eat the fish. Away from his wife's guarding glances, the stork dug his beak into the pan and got burnt to death. His wife came home to her husband's ashes scattered on the ground and broke into wails.

Contentment is the key to a happy life.

The Parrot and His Grandson

There was a *bahelia* who earned his livelihood by catching birds and selling them to the other villagers. Every day, he would go to the forest in the morning and return with his catch in the evening.

One summer day, the bahelia failed to catch any bird. He spread his nets several times and at several places in the jungle but the feathered denizens eluded him. 'The day has gone waste. I have nothing to take back home despite working so hard. How will I buy rice and vegetables to feed my children?' he thought anxiously.

Suddenly, his eyes fell on a small parrot pecking at the fruits scattered on the ground. The hunter caught the baby parrot, kept it in his bag and returned. 'It is a very small parrot. No one will buy it. I will put it in a cage. I will feed it and take care of it for a few days. It can fetch some money when it grows bigger. After all, something is better than nothing,' the bahelia murmured to himself. He knew that people would not eat a parrot. But they would keep him for company and entertainment. The small parrot had given him a reason to smile.

He came home and kept the parrot in a well-decorated cage. He put a bowlful of sprouts in the cage for the bird to eat. But the parrot had tears in his eyes. He was probably missing his family and home in the unfettered surroundings of the forest. He didn't eat.

On the other hand, the mother, father, grandfather and friends of the parrot got restless when they realized he was missing. They roamed in the woods, searching nest after nest, but failed to find the baby parrot. They didn't sleep the entire night, filled with remorse over losing a loved one from their flock.

Next morning, the baby parrot's grandfather—who had dodged many hunters in his long life—had an idea. He called the other parrots and suggested, 'Fly to different villages screeching "tein tein" loudly. My grandson will recognize our calls and will tweet back. That way, we can find out where he is.'

After suggesting so, the old parrot flew off with his flock. Incidentally, he sat on a tree close to the bahelia's home and began screeching. The baby parrot recognized his grandfather's voice and screeched from his cage that was suspended with a rope in the courtyard of the house.

The old parrot flew to his grandson. They continued screeching. The children gathered around to see another parrot near the one trapped in the cage. The baby parrot which earlier looked morose now danced in the cage, squawking. The children were delighted to see the scene.

After some time, the old parrot lost consciousness and fell on the ground. The villagers assumed that it was sunstroke. They sprinkled water on him and gave him some space to relax and get over his dizziness. A little later, the parrot got up and flew off.

As the villagers were discussing what had just happened,

the baby parrot inside the cage also fainted, with his feet up in the air. The hunter rushed to the cage, and carried the baby parrot out. Other family members sprinkled water on him and left him alone to get fresh air in the shade.

After half an hour or so, the baby parrot suddenly got up and flew off, screeching tein tein. The hunter was puzzled to see the baby parrot fly off. An elderly villager then explained, 'I guess the old parrot was the grandfather of the baby parrot. He came close to the baby parrot to teach him how to get out of the prison. The old parrot pretended to be unconscious and flew off, only to teach the baby parrot to do the same. The baby parrot learnt the lesson and eventually freed himself.'

Elders' wisdom teaches you a lot.

Animal Kingdom

How a Jackal Attained Pundit-hood

Once upon a time, a priest was passing through a forest in the fading light of the setting sun. Lions, tigers, wolves and other bloodhounds lurked in the woods. Scared, the priest quickened his pace in order to get out of the danger zone as soon as possible.

Suddenly, his eyes fell on a cage with a ferocious tiger confined in it. The priest became jittery. However, he recovered his senses when he realized that the tiger was caged and therefore could do no harm to him. Nonetheless, the sight of the tiger petrified him and he tried to walk past hurriedly.

As the tiger saw the priest hurry past, he cried, 'O priest! O my lord! O my saviour! Please have mercy on me.' This stopped the priest. Though scared, he thought it would be sinful and selfish to ignore the call of a distressed animal.

After a brief pause, the priest walked close to the cage and asked, 'What do you want?'

The tiger bewailed, 'Hunters caught me and locked me in this cage. Not a morsel of food has gone in my mouth for the last three days. I am dying of hunger.'

'What can I do for you?' the priest asked.

The tiger entreated, 'O my Lord, kind and pious! Please unlock the cage and free me. I will be greatly indebted to you if you set me free. It does not require much effort. Once I am free, I will set out to find a prey and satiate my hunger.'

The priest shuddered and said, 'Humans are your meal. You might devour me if I free you. How can I believe you won't eat me up?'

The tiger implored, 'O my Lord! Trust me. How can I eat a man who gives me my life back? The forest is full of animals I can prey on. I shall be beholden to you for the rest of my life for your kindness.'

The priest was confused. 'My faith teaches me to help someone in distress. But it is a tiger—a man-eater by nature. What should I do?' the priest tried to reason.

The tiger wailed even louder, 'I swear in the name of my siblings. I swear in the name of God. O my Lord, please free me from this cage so that I can eat something. My stomach is aching with hunger. Be kind to me, please save my life.'

The tiger's pitiable condition moved the priest. He shut his eyes and unlocked the cage with a prayer on his lips.

As soon as the tiger was out, he pounced on the priest with lightning speed. 'Don't move even an inch. I am hungry. First, I will devour you and then I will set out in search of other animals.'

The priest was stunned. He had goosebumps all over his body. With folded hands, he begged the tiger for mercy. He said, 'I have saved your life. Is this how you repay my kindness? I have children and a wife to take care of.'

The tiger roared, 'O priest. This is no place for preaching. I am hungry. The ethics of the forest do not allow me to go for another prey when there is one standing in front of me. We are not supposed to leave the prey in hand and go for the one in the bush. After all, I, too, am bound to follow certain rules.'

The priest continued, 'Don't be so unjust and unkind to me.'

But the tiger was in no mood to listen. 'Stop preaching. I am going to eat you.'

At that point, the priest had a brainwave, and hoping against hope, he decided to test it. He began, 'If you agree, I will give you certain suggestions before you eat me.'

'What suggestions? Tell me quickly,' the tiger roared.

The priest said, 'If you agree, I would like you to listen to the opinions of a few other forest dwellers before you eat me.'

'Okay. I have no objections,' the tiger consented.

In the meantime, a cow was passing by the spot where the tiger and the priest were talking. The priest said, 'O mother cow. Please listen to me.'

The cow said, 'What do you have to say?'

The priest said, 'This tiger was confined in the cage. I got him out of it and thus saved his life. Now, he wants to devour me. Is it righteous?'

The cow said, 'It is *kalyug*. No one is supposed to have gratitude for a favour done in this age. Take my case. My master fed me till I was young and produced milk for him. But as soon as I turned old and was unable to give him milk, he banished me from his house, leaving me to wander in this jungle. O priest, times are changing. If I speak in your favour, the tiger will devour me instead.'

The cow turned away and walked past listlessly.

Now, the tiger pounced on the priest. The priest folded his hands once again, begging, 'Listen to one more animal, please. I will not beg for more.'

The tiger allowed the priest to have one more opinion, telling him to hurry up. That is when a jackal happened to pass by. The priest shouted desperately, 'O jackal, O brother jackal...'

The jackal came, saying, 'What is the matter?'

The priest said, 'I freed this tiger from the cage. Now he is going to eat me.'

Interrupting the priest mid-sentence, the jackal scolded him. 'You are a liar of the first order. How can such a huge tiger be confined in such a small cage? I cannot believe it.'

The priest said, 'I am not lying. The tiger was trapped in this cage. I freed him.'

Wearing an expression of disbelief, the jackal turned his gaze on the tiger. The tiger corroborated the priest's claim, affirming that he was telling the truth. 'I was there in the cage,' he said.

The jackal retorted, 'I cannot believe this unless I see it with my own eyes.'

The boastful tiger took the jackal's words as a challenge and soon jumped into the cage, demonstrating how he had been trapped in it before. The clever jackal turned to the priest, commanding, 'O priest, what are you waiting for now? Hurry up! Lock the cage.'

The priest wasted no time in locking the cage. The cruel tiger was trapped once again, thanks to the jackal's tricks. The jackal flashed a triumphant smile. The priest heaved a huge sigh of relief and said, 'You are the real pundit, jackal. I am now passing on my pundit-hood to you.'

Both the jackal and the priest then resumed their journeys to their respective destinations. They lived happily ever after. It is for you to guess the fate that the tiger eventually met.

Wisdom and common sense are greater than valour.

The Boastful Jackal and the Timid Goat

Once upon a time there lived a she-goat and a she-dog in a village on the outskirts of a forest. While the goat lived on grass, the dog hunted on squirrels, rats and rabbits that were available in abundance in the nearby forest and also received leftover food occasionally from the villagers. Both the animals shared a friendly relationship.

After some time, the goat and the dog gave birth to two babies each. While the goat named her kids Bhal and Man, the she-dog named hers Chun and Mun. A few days after their birth, Bhal, Man, Chun and Mun became great friends. They would play, run and frolic all day when their mothers would be out in the forest in search of food.

There also lived a boastful jackal where the she-goat would go to graze the grass. He silently nursed the ambition to be called the 'king' but did not voice this as the forest also had lions, panthers and tigers—far superior in might and pedigree when compared to the jackal.

Despite the hesitation, the jackal wore a rosary of dead snails and crabs' bones and sat majestically on a raised platform in a corner—away from the tigers and lions—posing like a king.

27

He threw his weight around the weaker animals like goats and rabbits. One day, while grazing in the forest, the goat saw the jackal staring at her. She got scared.

Hurling abuses at the goat, the jackal said, 'O mean creature! Come close to me and press my feet.' The goat was too scared to refuse the jackal's command. She said, 'O king, my master! I will obey your command.' The jackal was thrilled to hear the goat refer to him as 'master' and 'king'.

The jackal asked the goat to chant a couplet in his praise. The couplet he suggested was:

Sone ke choutara chanana lipal baa,
Dono kane sonwa rajwa baithal baa.

(There is a golden platform plastered with
sandalwood paste,
The king, wearing gold rings in his ears, sits on it.)

The goat recited the couplet to satisfy the jackal's ego. But the jackal didn't stop there. He asked the goat, 'I have a plot of land. Plough it and grow wheat on it. We will distribute the produce equally when the crops are ready.' The goat, who was already petrified, meekly acquiesced to what the jackal commanded.

Next day, the goat requested the jackal, 'My master! Please accompany me to the land and help me plough it.' The jackal shot back, 'O petty creature! I am the king. I am not supposed to go to the farmland. Working on a farm is demeaning to my status.'

The goat worked hard on the field, furrowing, levelling it, and sowing wheat on it. A few months later, the wheat was ready for harvesting. The goat requested the jackal to accompany her so that she could harvest the crops and share the produce.

The jackal said, 'I am not a small king that I will accompany my *raiyat* on the farmland. Harvest the crop and bring it to me. I will distribute the produce.' The goat harvested the crops, carried it on her back to the jackal's burrow and thrashed it, sifting the wheat from the hay.

The jackal then took the wheat and said, 'You live on straws and hays. So, take the straws and hays. I will keep the grains.'

Helpless, the goat returned to the village, weeping. When Chun and Mun saw the goat weeping, they asked, 'Hi aunty! What happened? Why are you weeping?'

The goat narrated the story.

The pups were full of youthful exuberance. 'Don't weep, aunty. Take us to the place where the jackal lives and do what we tell you to do. We will teach the jackal a lesson or two.'

The she-dog was confident about her babies' prowess. She allowed her pups to accompany their goat aunty. As they reached the forest, they found the jackal sitting in the same style on the raised platform, waiting for the goat to come.

The dogs stayed behind, lurking in the bushes. They urged the goat to approach the jackal and recite the couplet they had taught her:

Maati ke choutara gobare lipal baa,
Duno kane ghongha siyara baithal baa.

(There is an earthen platform plastered with cow dung,
The jackal is sitting wearing crabs' bones in his ears.)

The verse was demeaning to the jackal. As the goat recited it, the jackal got furious and headed menacingly towards her. But soon, the pups came running, scaring the jackal, who hurried back in his burrow. The dogs sat at the burrow's opening, waiting for the jackal to come out. But the jackal stayed holed up. After a few hours, the jackal raised his head from the burrow to see if the dogs were still there.

But the dogs, who were waiting attentively at the burrow's mouth, struck him, slicing away the jackal's ears. While the jackal, bruised and earless, ran screaming in pain, the dogs came back with his ears to the village. Their mother said, 'I am happy that you have learnt to arrange for your breakfast. Enjoy the jackal's ears.'

The goat never saw the jackal again. Defeated by ignominy, the jackal had changed his spot. The goat grazed and lived merrily thereafter.

One should never bully others.

THE GREATEST FOLK TALES OF BIHAR

The Lioness and the Cow

There lived a priest in a certain village. He owned a cow that he cared for immensely and fed well. His children savoured the cow's milk. The priest had a happy family because of the abundance of milk from the bovine, gifts from disciples and foodgrains from his fertile fields.

But two consecutive spells of drought brought catastrophe on the villagers. The family of the priest ran short of food grains. The villagers battling famine were in no position to give anything to the priest whose wife and children were starving. He had also run short of feed and fodder for his cow.

A devout adherent of the message of the holy scriptures, the priest considered it sinful to keep the cow starving at his door and, thus, decided to sell it off.

The cow had been born and brought up at the priest's door. She was like a family member. The priest and his children loved her dearly and she was loyal to them. She sensed that the priest was thinking of selling her off due to poverty and she found it hard to adjust to the idea of living with another family.

'After all, everyone in the family is starving. I am ready to suffer from what others in the family are suffering from.

Why is the priest singling me out? He should have waited for the bad time to get over rather than deciding to send me to someone else's house,' the cow mused but she had no clue how to communicate what she was thinking to the priest.

On a day, when the priest was out in another village in search of a buyer, the cow silently broke away from her tether and strayed into the forest.

As she travelled in the deep woods, the cow encountered a lioness which said, 'Luck has smiled on me today by bringing you to me. I have a delicious cow to eat without much effort.'

The cow who had already lost interest in life after leaving her master's door said, 'I have no one to weep on my death. You can eat me. But I have a request to make before I surrender my body to you.'

The lioness asked her what the request was. The cow said, 'I am pregnant. I can feel my baby moving in my womb. As a mother, I request you to let me deliver my baby first and then do whatever you wish.'

Incidentally, the lioness, too, was pregnant. Her motherly instinct melted her heart, stopping her from eating the cow. After a few weeks, both the cow and the lioness gave birth. Since the lioness and the cow had lived together, suffering the pangs of pregnancy, they had become friends. As the days passed in togetherness, the lioness gave up the idea of eating the cow.

The lioness's cub and the cow's calf, too, became friends. They had fun and frolicked together, playing with each other in the vast expanse of the jungle. While the lioness hunted other animals to feast on with her cub, the cow and her calf grazed on the lush green grass in the forest. The animals resided thus in health and happiness.

One day, the lioness and the cow were drinking from the

same stream. The lioness tasted the cow's saliva, mixed in water. It was then that the lioness's carnivorous instinct fuelled her greed to eat the cow. She said, 'If the water mixed with your saliva is so tasty, how tasty will your flesh be? I find it hard to check the urge to eat you.'

The cow said, 'My udders are full of milk. Let me feed my son who must be hungry. Thereafter, I will hand myself over to you.'

The lioness permitted the cow to go and feed her baby. The cow broke into tears on seeing her baby who was hungry and desperately waiting for his mother. 'Why are you weeping, Mom?' the calf asked.

The cow replied, 'I am feeding you for the last time. Your lioness aunty has decided to eat me once I am done feeding you, my son.'

While feeding her baby, the cow released whatever milk there was in her udders and stored it in a pot. Then she left, telling the calf, 'Once the milk turns red you should understand that your lioness aunty has devoured me.'

After some time the milk turned red. Sensing that his mother had died, the calf wailed uncontrollably. The lioness's cub came to the calf, sad to see his friend in distress.

'Why are you weeping, my friend?' the cub asked.

'Lioness aunty has devoured my mom. I am an orphan now,' the calf said. Tied in the bond of friendship with the calf for so long, the cub was angry with his mother. He went to his mother and instantly killed her. The cub returned to the calf announcing, 'We both are motherless now. We will live together. I will protect you henceforth. You have nothing to worry about.'

Both the cub and the calf started living happily together. The cub tied a bell around the calf's neck, directing the latter,

'Ring the bell whenever you sense danger in your life. I will come running to save you.'

Once, while grazing somewhere in the forest, the calf shook his neck, ringing the bell. The lion came running to inquire, 'What happened? Why did you ring the bell?'

The calf said, 'Nothing worrisome. A mosquito bit me, driving me to shake my neck. That's how the bell rang.'

One day, a group of butchers was passing by the place where the calf was grazing. Enticed by his fleshy body, the butchers caught him and got ready to slaughter him. The calf repeatedly shook his neck, ringing the bell. But the cub who was engrossed in feasting on a delicious deer thought that the calf might have been disturbed by the mosquitoes once again, causing him to ring the bell.

After sometime, the bell stopped ringing. The cub now turned anxious, thinking that his friend had landed in some real trouble. He ran to the place from where the jingles of the bell were coming. As he reached the spot, he saw that the butchers were roasting the calf on a fire to feast on him.

Gripped by guilt at the loss of his dearest friend, the cub, too, jumped into the fire, ending his life.

Never be frivolous with friendships.

How the Jackal Got Lessons in Picking Fruits

There lived a jackal and a monkey in a certain forest full of palm trees laden with fruits. The ripened palm fruits contained yellow jelly that was sweet and delicious. Once the outer layer of the fruit was skinned off, it was left with the fibrous parts full with mouthwatering jelly.

The monkey—a dexterous treehopper—climbed the trees and ate the delicious fruits. The jackal loitering under the palm trees would eat the leftover fruits sucked and thrown by the monkey. The jackal loved eating what was also known as ice apple but never got a full fruit to eat.

One day, the monkey was on the tree eating the fruit and the jackal was standing under the tall tree. The jackal said, 'Brother monkey! It would be really nice of you if you could throw a full-sized fruit to me. I will be very happy to get a full-sized ice apple.'

The monkey, enjoying the fruit, said, 'Why should you depend on me to throw the fruit? The ripened fruits fall on their own every day. The only thing you have to do is to stand under the tree and wait for the fruit to drop. You will get it.'

Early next morning, the jackal went to the tree. A big fruit fell on his head, hurting him badly. The jackal twisted in pain and ran away, howling. He rested in the shade of a bush for a few days and decided never to go near the palm tree again.

Eventually, the jackal moved to the nearby village full of mango orchards. It was the season for the mangoes to ripen. The jackal would go to one of the orchards at night when its owner would be asleep and eat the mangoes to his heart's content, scattering the leftovers in the process.

The jackal had a nice time for many days. But as it happened, a big bee was stuck in one of the mangoes that the jackal picked up to eat. The bee stung him in the mouth as the jackal began chewing it. Hurt, the jackal let out a howl, turning and twisting. The jackal's loud howl awoke the orchard owner who ran to chase the animal out with a club in his hands.

The jackal somehow managed to flee. But his mouth swelled. It did not open for days. His other jackal friends gathered around to lick the wound and cured it in a few days.

Once the jackal recovered fully, he took a life-changing vow:

Jingi jiayon ta tad na jaon
Jaiebo karab ta aam na khaon
Khaebo karab ta tapka chhor ke lokua khaon

(I won't go near a palm tree ever.
I won't eat the mangoes dropped in my absence and scattered on the ground.
If at all I eat, I will eat a freshly dropped mango.)

Never take shortcuts; fruits attained
without efforts can harm you.

The Jackal and the Camel

There lived a jackal and camel in a forest. They were very friendly with each other. The jackal was small but swift. The camel was big and heavy but slow and dull.

Once, when the sun set and dusk descended, the jackal told the camel, 'My friend! There are plenty of watermelons and cucumbers growing in the field a few miles away. If we go there we will have tasty cucumbers and watermelons to eat.'

'Your idea is great. Let us go to the field as soon as possible,' the camel concurred. The animals then proceeded to the field.

As they travelled some distance, they found a river on the way. 'I am scared of entering the river. I am a small animal. How can I cross the river? I might drown in the river's swirling currents,' the jackal said.

The camel offered, 'Don't worry. Ride on my back. I will carry you and swim across the river.' The jackal mounted the camel and they swam across the river together.

The riverbank opened to a sprawling field full of mouthwatering watermelons and cucumbers. The animals got busy enjoying the luscious crops. The jackal's tiny stomach was full soon but the camel, with a large stomach, was taking his time.

The jackal said, 'My stomach is full and I feel like howling "huaa huaa" now.'

The camel pleaded, 'Please don't do it right now. Let me fill my stomach too. Once we get out of the field you can do whatever you want.'

But the jackal, unable to control his temptation, howled at the top of his voice. The landowner, who was sleeping in a hut nearby, to guard his crops, rushed to see the animals feasting on his crops; with a club in his hand. The jackal swiftly fled away but the camel, slow on his feet, bore the farmer's brunt.

The farmer rained his club on the camel. The camel, bruised and battered, wobbled out of the field, walking slowly on his return journey.

The jackal was waiting at the riverbank for the camel to arrive and carry him across. When the camel—grimacing in pain—reached there, the jackal jumped onto the camel's back and pleaded the latter to carry him along.

The camel did not object initially but as he reached midstream, he said, 'My back and limbs are paining. I feel the urge to stretch to lessen the excruciating pain I am undergoing.'

The jackal got frightened and pleaded, 'My dear friend! You know how small I am. Once you begin stretching, I will lose my balance and drown.' The camel said, 'Why should I care for your life? Had you cared for me, you would not have howled, thus awaking the farmer and getting me beaten up. Now I will stretch in the water to heal myself without thinking of you.'

Thereafter, the camel began stretching. He turned upside

down. He plunged his back in the stream and turned his neck up and down. Unable to hold on, the jackal lost his balance and drowned in the river.

The camel then swam back to the forest alone.

Never breach a friend's trust.

The Donkey and the Dog

There lived a dhobi. He had a donkey and a dog. The two animals were loyal to him. The donkey would carry bundles of clothes to the riverbank and get them back. The dog would bark to scare away the thieves and enemies, thus guarding his master's belongings.

Once, the dhobi didn't offer food to the dog and went to sleep. The dog got hungry. As the night advanced, the canine's stomach ached in hunger. Sleep eluded him and he lay down in a corner, sobbing.

The darkness of the night deepened. Other villagers too had slept. An eerie silence gripped the atmosphere. Suddenly, a thief tiptoed into the dhobi's hut but the dog kept silent.

The donkey which was standing at the door questioned the dog's conduct. 'Why are you not barking at the thief that has just entered our master's home? If you don't bark, the master will keep sleeping and the thief will run away with his belongings.'

The dog said, 'Why should I bark? The master didn't offer me food tonight. Let him suffer for starving me.'

But the donkey said, 'Don't be ungrateful to our master. After all, he has raised you, fed you and sheltered you for years. You shouldn't shirk your duty now when a thief has entered the house. The master's failure to give you food once shouldn't deter you from barking when it is needed the most.'

The dog retorted angrily, 'Keep shut. Don't give me sermons on how to do my duty. Had you been hungry like me, you would have understood how hard it is to keep the sense of duty on an empty stomach.'

But the donkey was restless. He wanted his master to get up and chase the thief before the latter eloped with his belongings. He said, 'If you don't bark, I will bray to awake the master.'

The dog shot back, 'You stupid donkey! You should do what you are supposed to do. You shouldn't poke your nose in others' business.'

But the donkey thought it would be dishonest to listen to the dog. He started braying 'dhenchooo dhenchooo' at the top of his voice.

The dhobi was tired after pounding the clothes on the riverbank the entire day and was deep in sleep. Robbed of his sleep at an odd time, he picked up the club he used to pound clothes and began beating the donkey.

Seeing the dhobi awake, the thief fled with whatever he had picked up. The donkey ended up with his limbs fractured and back bruised. The dog mocked the poor donkey, 'You are stupid! I had asked you not to go out of your way. The rule of the game is to mind one's own business and never enter another's domain. You have suffered for acting foolishly.'

The true sufferer, however, was the dhobi, who had his belongings stolen from him and was left with a wounded donkey, unable to carry the clothes to the riverbank the next day.

One should mind one's own business.

How the Jackal Preyed on the Goat

A hungry jackal was in search of food in a forest. He was looking for rabbits, rats or squirrels to catch as he couldn't prey on bigger animals. But the smaller animals were eluding him. His roving eyes fell on a goat grazing nearby. His mouth began watering at the mere sight of the goat. But the goat was fleshy and well-built. It had sharp horns and a flowing black beard. The jackal feared attacking the goat.

'It is better to stay hungry than to try and catch a sharp-horned goat which might tear my stomach,' the jackal thought. But his clever mind was already at work. He lurked in the bushes and began thinking of tricks to trap the goat, which had no inkling of the presence of a predator around.

With her stomach full of lush green grass, the goat travelled to a nearby pond to drink water. The cunning jackal now had an idea. He walked stealthily to the edge of the pond and urinated on the path that the goat would take to return.

The jackal's discharge loosened the soil, making it slippery. The trick worked—when the goat tried to return, her foot slipped and she fell in the pond. As the goat fell, the jackal urinated more, making the mud on the edge slippery. The goat made frenzied attempts to get out of the pond but her repeated efforts failed as her feet could not find a footing in the muddy soil.

Struggling in the water for some time, the goat drowned and died.

But the jackal was far from achieving his mission. He had no idea how to fish the goat out of the pond. He adopted another trick. He saw some farmers harvesting gram in the nearby field. He went near the field, howling 'hua hua' and tried to repeatedly catch their attention.

The farmers thought that the jackal was suggesting something about the pond. They went to the pond, only to find the body of the goat floating on its surface. They soon fished the goat out. They lit a fire, roasted the goat and began feasting on it.

The hungry jackal sulked in a corner, pondering, 'I worked so hard to kill the goat. It was my prey. How unfortunate I am. The farmers are feasting on the labour of my love and I can't eat even a portion of the meat.'

Once again, he had a brainwave. He stealthily picked up the wood which had caught fire and threw it in the field. The crops caught fire. As the farmers noticed the inferno leaping in the field, they left the meat and rushed to save their crop. Finally, the jackal dragged the roasted goat into the bushes and ate it, satiating his hunger.

Try and try, and you will succeed.

Survival in the Wild

The Poor Brahmin and His Seven Daughters

There lived a poor Brahmin with his wife and seven daughters in a village. He lived on charity. Occasionally, he got some grains and clothes in lieu of the religious rituals he performed at the villagers' home. But the villagers, too, were poor. They had small holdings. Some of them raised cattle to supplement their income. But by and large, they had a hand-to-mouth existence.

The priest's poverty grew as his daughters grew in age and size. Their meals increased and they needed more clothes to wear. The priest spent all his days going from door to door for alms. Still, he and his wife had to sleep without eating anything on certain nights as they had nothing left after feeding their daughters.

One day, the Brahmin felt the urge to eat kheer and expressed his desire to his wife. The wife who was fully devoted to her husband was eager to fulfil his wish. But she had no means to do it as she only had whatever her husband brought home as alms. 'I suggest you go to the cattle-rearing farmers and beg for some milk. Arrange for some rice and sugar. I will be happy to cook kheer for you,' she said, looking lovingly at her husband.

The Brahmin got up early the next morning and set out to beg in distant villages. He managed some milk, sugar and rice at the end of the day. When he brought the items home, his wife measured them and said, 'The ingredients are not enough to prepare kheer for the entire family. I will make our daughters sleep after feeding them something else. Then I will cook kheer so that you can have it to your heart's content.'

The poverty-stricken Brahmin agreed to his wife's proposal. She cooked kheer late in the night when her children were asleep and offered it to her husband. But as the priest had the first spoon, the youngest daughter woke up. Her mother murmured, 'Don't make any sound. Come slowly to us.' The priest put a spoonful of kheer in his daughter's mouth, asking her to go to sleep again. And then, he thought of eating the remaining kheer.

But before he could do that, the second daughter got up. Wobbling, she came to her parents and asked them to feed her what they had fed her sister. The priest fed her too. One by one, the other five woke up too and the priest ended up feeding the entire bowl of kheer to his children. He and his wife had to sleep without eating anything that night too.

The Brahmin was upset the next morning. 'It is hard to gather enough food for my daughters every day. How will I marry them off when they attain the marriageable age?' he pondered. The thought depressed him and he decided to get rid of his children.

He told them about a tree laden with ripe berries in the forest and suggested that if they accompanied him, he would make them eat the luscious fruits. The possibility of getting tasty fruits to eat lit up the girls' face. They merrily accompanied their father to the forest.

As the Brahmin reached the forest, he shook the tree's

branches. The fruits one by one dropped and scattered on the ground. The girls got engrossed in eating the berries. The priest, on the pretext of attending the call of nature, vanished from the site.

When the girls were full, they looked for their father. Soon, the sun would set. The girls faced the threat of attacks from tigers, lions and panthers in the forest. They called out to their father but got no response. Some of them broke into wails.

The eldest sister was mature. 'It appears that our father will not return to take us home. We should look for someplace so that we can save our lives from the animals,' she suggested. Wandering, the seven sisters came across an old house abandoned in the forest. The girls entered the house, only to find seven stoves that had seven pans full of boiled milk with thick layers of cream.

The girls ate the delicious cream and huddled in an isolated corner of the house. After some time, seven black bears entered with seven buffaloes. As a matter of routine, the bears always milked their buffaloes and put the milk to boil on the stove every morning. They would then eat the cream and drink the milk when they returned with their cattle in the evening.

After tying up the buffaloes, the bears went to the stoves but to their surprise they found the cream missing. Pondering over how the cream had vanished from the surface of the milk, the bears drank the cream-less milk and slept.

Next morning, they milked their buffaloes, poured the milk in the pans and put them on the stoves for boiling before going out with their buffaloes in the forest to graze them.

However, the next day too, the girls ate the cream, leaving the cream-less milk for the bears. This continued for seven to eight days. The bears searched for the 'thieves' who were stealing their cream regularly but failed to find anyone.

Eventually, they decided that some invisible ghosts had entered their house.

'The ghosts are eating our cream every day. They might devour us all one day,' the eldest bear feared. The other bears concurred and they all fled from the house leaving their buffaloes.

After they left, the sisters had a great time. They herded the buffaloes that grazed in the forest. They milked them, and prepared cream and yoghurt to eat. In a few days, the girls became healthy and began living merrily. They almost forgot their parents and their days of poverty.

Meanwhile, the priest's conscience was pricking him. He often thought of his daughters and the way he had abandoned them. One day, he proceeded to the forest to search for his daughters. Wandering, he succeeded in locating the house where the girls lived. He got excited to see his daughters happy and healthy. He embraced them and broke into tears.

The daughters, too, were happy to meet their father after a long time. The priest then begged them, 'Forgive me for leaving you all alone. Let us go home. Your mother will be happy to see you all after such a long time.'

Initially, the girls did not like the idea of going back. But the emotional persuasion by their father made them relent. They reached home with the seven buffaloes. The priest's fortune turned overnight. Rich with seven buffaloes, he sold milk, curd and yoghurt, earning immense wealth.

Over the years, the priest got richer and married off his daughters to prosperous grooms. He gave up beggary and lived happily thereafter.

You never know when and how your luck will smile on you.

The Fear of Tiptipwa

O nce upon a time, there lived an old woman in a forest. She possessed a horse which she loved like her son. Grazing on the lush green grass in the forest, the horse had become healthy and robust. The woman would tie it to a post under a banyan tree near her hut and massage its back and limbs before going to sleep at night. The horse got sumptuous food and love every day and the woman had a companion in the desolate forest.

One day, a thief saw the horse and decided to steal it. A tiger, too, came to know about the horse living under the woman's patronage and thought of feeding on it. Though the thief and the tiger had a common cause, they were unknown to each other and were unaware of each other's plan.

The weather changed abruptly the next day. A stormy blanket of cloud shrouded the forest after sunset. Flashes of lightning ripped through the inky atmosphere. The horse was sitting near the hut where the woman was holed up.

The thief and the tiger found the scary weather appropriate to operate in. They stealthily reached the hut at the same time—although separately. They prepared to strike the horse from two separate corners in opposite directions.

Though the tiger and the thief hadn't seen each other, the woman had sensed the presence of the enemies around. Having lived in the jungle for years, the old woman had learnt how to deal with inclement weather and predators. Silently resting in her hut, she was cognizant of her horse's safety and security.

The tiger and the thief were focused on their prey. They were waiting for a brilliant flash of lightning to rip through the dark before they made their move. Suddenly, the old woman chanted in a loud voice, 'Neither do I fear a tiger nor a thief. What I am actually frightened of is Tiptipwa.'

The tiger and the thief got confused when they heard the woman's chant. They got distracted from their prey. 'What is Tiptipwa? The woman fears Tiptipwa more than me. This means that Tiptipwa is either a more dreaded animal than me or a monster or a ghost,' the tiger mused. The thief, on the other hand, thought that Tiptipwa might be some dangerous species and got frightened.

Just then, lightning forked through the graphite night, enabling the tiger and the thief to see the horse and strike. The tiger jumped on the horse. Simultaneously, the thief threw a strap aiming at the neck of the horse. But instead, the strap fell around the neck of the tiger that had jumped on the horse.

The tiger, full of doubt about Tiptipwa, thought that it was Tiptipwa that had entrapped him. He got scared. The night had gotten inky again and nothing was visible in the darkness. Meanwhile, the thief thought that he had entrapped the horse. Thinking that the tiger was the horse, he mounted it.

When the thief tried to climb it, the tiger thought that it was Tiptipwa that had overpowered him and tried to break free. When lightning struck again, the thief saw that he was sitting on the tiger and dismounted hurriedly. He entered a hole in a tree to save himself.

The tiger ran and kept running till dawn broke. When a jackal saw the tiger running, he asked, 'O uncle! Why are you so nervous? You are our master. If you get so frightened, what will happen to us?'

The tiger paused, saying, 'O jackal! Tiptipwa had attacked me. He spared me only a little while ago and is hiding in that tree.' The jackal quipped, 'Don't worry, my master. Let us go together to get Tiptipwa out of the hole. We should kill and feast on him.'

The tiger and the jackal reached the tree in which the thief was holed up. The tiger asked the jackal to put his tail in the tree's hole to scare Tiptipwa out. But as the jackal moved his tail, the thief caught it and began pulling it with both his hands.

The jackal asked the tiger to shove his paw into the hole to scare Tiptipwa so that he would loosen his grip on the tail. But the tiger who was already scared fled. The thief eventually pulled out the jackal's tail from his body.

Wounded and stripped of his tail the jackal loitered in the forest pitiably for days. With time, his wounds healed but he was the subject of ridicule in his community. After many days, he was blessed with happiness when a she-jackal fell in love with him and they got married.

They bore five cubs after some time. Having lived together for long, the she-jackal asked her husband to take her to his home. The jackal took his wife and kids to a tunnel in the hills and described it as his home to his family.

As the she-jackal entered the burrow, she encountered an unusual smell. 'The burrow is filled with the smell of tigers. How can it be your home?' she asked her husband.

The jackal shot back, 'Honey, it is the smell of the tigers' meat. I hunt the tigers and eat their meat.'

Soon after they settled in the burrow, the jackal saw a tiger approaching them. It was the same tiger for whom the jackal had lost his tail. The jackal got scared and revealed the truth to his wife.

But the she-jackal was cleverer. She proposed, 'I will beat up the children, making them weep loudly. I will say that the kids are weeping for tiger's flesh. You should then ask the kids to stop making noise so that the tiger does not run away.'

The she-jackal beat up her children, making them cry, and the jackal asked them to keep quiet so that the tiger wouldn't run away—just like they had planned.

'The cubs are weeping for my meat! It might be another ploy of Tiptipwa to trap me,' the tiger thought and fled.

On his way, he encountered another jackal who said, 'Don't worry. The jackals who have occupied your home are my family friends. I will get them to vacate your den.'

The scared tiger tied the jackal to his hind legs and went to the burrow dragging him along. As the jackals in the burrow saw the tiger coming with another jackal, the she-jackal suggested to her husband, 'You should get angry at the jackal and say, "I had paid you to bring five tigers but you have brought only one. I won't spare you."'

The jackal did exactly that. The petrified tiger fled again, dragging the jackal with him. On the other hand, the jackal that had been stripped of his tail, lived happily with his family thereafter.

Being street-smart helps in every situation.

The Cobbler and the Washerman

There lived two poor youths called Kallu and Mallu. They belonged to the Chamar and Dhobi castes, respectively, and lived in a village largely inhabited by Dalits. According to his traditional vocation, Kallu was supposed to make shoes and sell them for a living. But he was too poor to buy the tools and leather required to make shoes. Moreover, there wasn't much demand for shoes as most villagers walked barefoot. They couldn't afford the 'luxury' of wearing shoes.

Mallu, somehow, carried on with his caste's vocation. He washed others' clothes and raised donkeys to carry the linens and detergent. Kallu, on the other hand, managed by collecting firewood from the nearby forest and bartering it for grains in the village.

One day, he encountered a tiger in the forest. But Kallu was very wise. As he saw the tiger, he sat on his knees, beseeching the animal, 'I salute you, tiger uncle.'

The tiger mused, 'After a long time, I have gotten a young man—fleshy and yummy. But he has saluted me and has now tied me in a bond. It will amount to a big sin if I eat him.'

While the tiger was in a contemplative mood, Kallu turned

55

more docile and said, 'Tiger uncle, you must get hurt when thorns prick your paws while travelling in the rugged terrains. I will gift you two pairs of shoes to fit your four paws. Please come after sunset and wait in the bushes behind my hut. I will deliver you the shoes that will provide you comfort when you run and hunt animals.'

The tiger agreed and Kallu, having managed to ward off the imminent danger to his life, hurried back to his hut. But the tiger, driven by the desire to wear shoes, came when darkness descended and hid in the bushes behind Kallu's hut. In the meantime, Mallu came looking for his donkey, which had strayed in the dark.

'Have you seen my donkey?' Mallu called out to Kallu. It was drizzling, making the night darker. From his hut, Kallu said, 'I just heard some commotion in the bushes. See if your donkey is there.'

Mallu tiptoed into the bushes. He stumbled upon the tiger and thinking it was his donkey in the dark, he mounted it. 'Whoa donkey...,' Mallu shouted, goading the tiger with a long whip he was holding. The tiger got confused. He began running towards the forest with Mallu on his back, whipping him in the same way he would whip his donkey.

Having travelled for a few yards, Mallu noticed in a sudden flash of lightning that he was sitting on a tiger. He cautiously disembarked from the tiger's back and hid inside the hole of a big banyan tree on the way. The tiger, running in panic, reached the forest.

A jackal, seeing the frightened tiger asked, 'What happened, brother tiger? Why are you so nervous?'

The tiger said, 'It was an unusually calamitous time for me. A ghost climbed onto my back and whipped me relentlessly. I have never experienced such horror in the past.'

'Where is that ghost?'

'He is inside the wide hole of that banyan tree,' the tiger said, gesturing towards the tree.

The jackal said, 'The ghost has frightened our master. It is a bad thing. If the ghost is allowed to escape unhurt he will develop the habit of preying on all of us. Let me go and drag him out of the hole.'

The tiger warned him, 'You foolish jackal! He has driven me in panic. What do you think of yourself? Don't overestimate yourself.'

But the boastful jackal ignored the tiger's warning and headed towards the banyan tree. Having reached there, he raised his long tail and put it in the hole to scare the 'ghost'. Mallu who was ensconced inside caught the jackal's tail in his vicious grip and began pulling it. The jackal, too, pulled his body in the opposite direction. In the tug of war, the jackal's tail got uprooted and was left in Mallu's grip.

The jackals crying 'hua hua' in a fit of pain reached the tiger and announced, 'He is not a ghost. He is actually a tail puller. He has pulled my tail off.'

The tiger reprimanded the jackal and said, 'You foolish creature! I warned you against that beast. But you disobeyed my command. Now he has robbed you of your tail, and you'll have to live without it forever.'

After quarrelling for some time, both the tiger and the jackal settled down, turning contemplative. The tiger said, 'It is a difficult situation. A ghost is lurking nearby. He might devour all the members of our clan one by one.'

Bruised and panicked, the jackal asked, 'My elder brother! Tell us what we should do to get rid of the monster.' The tiger ordered the jackal to gather all the animals—lions, dogs, cats, leopards, bears and panthers. 'We should collectively go and uproot the tree, breaking it into pieces and forcing the ghost to get out. Then we will kill him and feast on his flesh.'

All the animals gathered around the tree and smashed it. Once Mallu came out, all the animals headed to tear him down and devour him.

'I will kill him first,' the tiger roared.

The lion said, 'I am the king of the forest. I will kill him first.' The leopards and panthers began fighting to be the first to kill Mallu.

Sensing danger to his life, Mallu thought of an idea. With folded hands, he begged the animals, 'You are too many in number. You won't even get a mouthful of me each if you kill me. I suggest you bring flour, sugar and ghee, which you can find in abundance by breaking into the homes of people living nearby. I will prepare tasty *malpua*s and give each of you as many as you want. It will also be a change of taste for all of you.'

The animals agreed. They arranged plenty of flour, sugar and ghee. Mallu prepared the malpuas and began throwing them towards the animals. But the bigger animals—tigers, lions and leopards—ate them all while the smaller and frailer ones like jackals and cats did not get even a piece to taste.

Now, Mallu suggested, 'Bring me a small rope. I will tie all of you with the rope in a row and distribute the malpuas amongst you equally. This way all of you will get your share.'

The animals soon brought the rope and allowed themselves to be tied. Now, Mallu used the ghee that was boiling in a huge frying pan. He poured hot ghee one by one in the mouths of the tied animals. They failed to bear the heat and died.

Mallu rushed to Kallu to narrate his feat. On hearing the story, Kallu hurried to the forest with his tools and was overjoyed to see a pile of dead animals. He skinned them, collecting enough leather to make plenty of shoes to sell in the market. He involved Mallu in the enterprise as well. Thereafter, Mallu and Kallu shared the profits among themselves and lived merrily.

If you use wisdom to overcome odds, you will always succeed.

Folk Fun

The Gossiper

There lived a gossiper in a certain village. He was notorious for spreading rumours about others. But the villagers loved him, for he was an excellent entertainer.

One day, the gossiper went to a confectioner in the neighbourhood. The confectioner was sitting idle, for he had no customers to deal with at that particular time. The gossiper sat on his haunches near him.

'I am getting bored as I have no work to do. Tell me some gossip to entertain me,' the confectioner told the gossiper.

The gossiper said, 'I am not in a good mood right now. I am really hurt by your wife's conduct.'

'What happened?' the confectioner asked.

'I just saw your wife entering a sugar cane field with another man,' the gossiper said, looking at the vast swathe of sugar cane crop near the confectioner's house.

Having learnt that his wife had stepped out with another man, the confectioner got furious. He picked up a stick and ran towards the sugar cane field in search of his 'cheating' wife.

Subsequently, the confectioner's wife came out of the house, only to see the gossiper sitting alone near the door.

'Where is my husband?' she enquired.

The gossiper said, 'I just saw him entering the sugar cane field with another woman who was more beautiful than you.'

Angered by his words, the woman soon whipped out a broom and ran towards the sugar cane field in search of her 'cheating' husband.

Searching for each other, both the husband and the wife found themselves face-to-face in the middle of the thick sugar cane field. The wife, threatening the husband with the broom, said, 'Am I dead? Why are you loitering around with another woman?'

The husband shot back, 'You should ask yourself this question! Why did you enter the sugar cane field with another man?'

But there was neither a man nor a woman around other than the husband and wife, now engaged in an angry spat. Soon, they realized that they had fallen prey to the pranks of the gossiper.

The husband quipped, 'It appears that the gossiper has pulled a fast one on us.' The wife agreed, resolving the issue with her husband.

The confectioner then proposed, 'We have run through dirt and cow dung littered in the field. Let us go and take a bath in the nearby river to clean ourselves. Then we will go home.' Thus, the husband and wife went to the river to freshen up.

In the meantime, the confectioner's brother-in-law came to his door. Seeing the gossiper sitting there, the relative asked about his sister and brother-in-law.

With a sad face, the gossiper said, 'The confectioner and his wife had a son, right? The small boy died all of a sudden. They have gone to consign the body in the river. I am here to guard their house and attend to their relatives in their absence.'

Hearing this, the man broke into tears and ran towards the river. He saw his sister and brother-in-law coming from a distance. He wailed loudly.

'Why are you weeping so uncontrollably?' asked his brother-in-law. The man replied, 'The news of my nephew's death has jolted me. The gossiper has told me everything.'

The woman said, 'My son has gone to school. Nothing bad has happened to him.' The relative heaved a sigh of relief.

As they reached home, they saw the gossiper sitting nonchalantly at their door. Furious with the gossiper, the confectioner brandished his stick and asked, 'You stupid gossiper! You played all sorts of pranks on us, you made our lives hell. Why did you do so?'

The gossiper smirked, 'You were the one who asked me to gossip.'

Gossiping is a futile exercise and a waste of time.

The Simpleton

There lived a poor woman and her son named Sudhua in a village called Bhalai-Bhadaura. 'Sudhua' is also a slang in the local Bhojpuri-Magahi dialect, which means a simpleton.

Sudhua was a pampered child. The doting mother showered all her love on her only son. She did not let him toil in the fields. Too much pampering, perhaps, had rendered Sudhua downright naïve.

Even though he was fifteen, his mother would guard him against the kitchen fire. She would help him wear his clothes and feed him rice soaked in milk and jaggery from her own hands, which he relished. He played with marbles amongst the younger children on the streets and stayed away from the company of elders.

One day, Sudhua insisted on going to meet his grandmother, who lived in another village, five miles away. His mother objected, saying, 'You are a kid. You have never been away from home. You will stray on the way. I will not let you go that far.'

But Sudhua was adamant. 'I am not a breast-sucking kid! I go to urinate and defecate on my own. I bathe on my own.

Why can't I go to my grandmother's home on my own?' he argued.

The benign mother finally agreed. She promised to let him go the next morning. Restless as he was to visit his grandmother, Sudhua had a disturbed sleep. He dreamed about the time his grandmother had given him a hand-sewn doll to play with when he had last visited her with his mother.

Sudhua got up early the next morning and got ready to leave for his grandmother's village. He asked his mother about the route to follow. The mother showed him the path that originated from his village. 'Walk straight to your nose on the pathway. Don't deviate. You will reach there in three or four hours,' the mother said, indicating the path with her index finger.

Sudhua set out on the journey.

Having walked for a few hours, he saw a tall palm tree right before his nose. He got confused. 'My mother has asked to move straight. The palm tree is there in front of my nose. What should I do now?' Sudhua thought.

He decided to climb the tree and get down on the other side to resume his journey straight to his nose. He climbed the palm tree. The leaves had formed a canopy-like structure on the top. In an attempt to get down, Sudhua caught hold of the tree's fan-like canopy and suspended himself to the other side. But he was unable to clutch the palm tree's trunk which was the only way to crawl his way down. He lay suspended in the air, looking for someone to rescue him.

Sudhua saw a man on an elephant at some distance. He yelled, 'Whoa, Uncle mahout! Help me, please.' The mahout got the elephant near the tree and stood on its back. He caught hold of Sudhua's feet to help him come down. In the meantime, the leaves swished noisily, disturbing the elephant, which moved a little, leaving the mahout tied to the boy's feet. Now Sudhua was hanging on to the tree's leaves and the mahout was hanging on to Sudhua's feet.

Then they saw a man on a camel's back roaming in the nearby field. They drew the camel rider's attention to themselves. The camel rider, too, came to help them. He held the mahout's feet to help them get down. But the leaves rustled again, thus disturbing the camel, which moved ahead. Now Sudhua, the mahout and the camel rider lay suspended in the air together.

They saw a courtesan riding in a chariot to perform at a king's palace. They called out to the courtesan. She brought her chariot below the hanging men to rescue them. But the situation that had caused the elephant and the camel happened to the horses as well. The horses moved with the chariot. The courtesan who had clutched the camel rider's feet, too, lay suspended in the air with them.

Helpless, the four of them broke into a quarrel, abusing each other. Sudhua thought of an idea to restore peace. He suggested to the courtesan, 'You are a good singer. If you sing we will get entertained. Please sing so that the quarrel ends.'

The courtesan got furious. 'Our lives are in danger and you are suggesting me to sing? You are a real dolt!'

Sudhua said, 'Don't get angry. I know how to sing *biraha*. Don't sing if you are in a foul mood. I am going to sing biraha.'

Biraha is a form of song which requires the singer to plug both his ears with his fingers. Sudhua left the leaves he was holding to plug his ears and all four fell to the ground. The camel rider and mahout were tough and strong. After grimacing for a while, they got up and walked away. But the courtesan had her limbs wounded.

Sudhua, too, tried to get up and walk. The courtesan

screamed, 'You can't leave me in such a situation. I am wounded because of you. You will have go to a shop, buy oil for me and massage my limbs so that I am fit and able to move again.'

Sudhua agreed to fetch oil and massage the courtesan's wounded limbs. The courtesan placed a coin on Sudhua's palm. He went to the shop with a bowl and asked the shopkeeper to give him oil worth the coin. The shopkeeper filled the bowl with oil.

Sudhua then asked for more oil. The shopkeeper screamed back, 'Your bowl is full. Where will you keep more oil?'

Sudhua then turned the pot upside down and asked the shopkeeper to pour oil on the back of the pot. The shopkeeper realized that the buyer was a fool and tried to get rid of him. He poured oil on the back of the pot and asked Sudhua to leave.

Sudhua came back to the courtesan with some oil stuck on the pot. He offered to massage her wounded limbs with the scanty oil. The courtesan was livid again. 'You spent the money and did not even get the oil. What will you massage me with now? Get lost. Leave me to my own fate. You have caused more harm than good.'

Sudhua did not think twice. He left the place. But he was confused about the way, so he turned around and returned home.

Never trust a fool.

Munshiji and Raiji

There lived a munshi in a certain village during the British rule in India.

The post of a munshi was a prestigious position at the village level. The job involved collecting land taxes from the landholders and depositing them with the district collectors, who were largely Englishmen. The munshi also maintained the accounts of land and taxes. The villagers would refer to him as Munshiji, as a mark of respect for his position.

The munshi invariably belonged to the Kayastha caste, which had education-related jobs—mainly accounting and clerkship in the villages during the British rule. The Kayasthas by virtue of their literacy also handled the accountancy work during the Mughal rule that preceded the British Raj.

True to his caste, Munshiji used to collect taxes from the farmers and deposit them to the office of the district collector. Deep within their hearts, the villagers detested the munshi for his arrival at their door meant they would have to cough up cash, which was hard to come by. But they had to deal with him because he had an integral role in the civil administration of the village.

One day, Munshiji arrived at the door of Raiji—a Yadav cultivator—and informed him that the latter had not paid taxes for the last four years. 'You are required to pay the accumulated taxes in one go now. I will give you a receipt once you pay me the full amount. Otherwise, you can land in trouble,' the munshi said.

The Yadavs were a lathi-wielding community known for their unruly ways in that era. They were largely illiterate and earned their livelihood by herding cattle and farming. They had a penchant for bodybuilding and wrestling, and used their lathis to solve any problem they faced.

When the munshi asked for the taxes, Raiji asked the munshi to look at his well-oiled lathi. Lifting the ten-foot-long bamboo baton on his shoulder, Raiji said, 'I won't pay the taxes. I haven't paid for four years. But you have to give me the tax receipt. If you don't give me the receipt, I won't allow you to move an inch from here.'

The munshi—sharp with his tongue but frail in physique—was in a tight spot now. In his soft and sober tone, he pleaded, 'It is hard for you or anyone else to digest the government's tax. If you don't pay the tax you might be charged with defalcating government money, thus landing in jail.'

Raiji waved his lathi, and in his rough voice, he said, 'Write the receipt without any delay and give it to me. Deposit the money to the collector from your salary. Otherwise, my lathi will start working. You can understand what will happen to your limbs once my lathi gets started.'

The munshi sensed danger. He thought of using a wise trick that would save his life as well as help him collect taxes from the unruly farmer. He wrote 'Lathi *ka hathe malgujari bewak* (Receipt given against power of club)' on a piece of paper and gave it to Raiji.

The illiterate Yadav twirled his moustache, kept the piece of paper and whispered boastfully, 'Lathi *se tou bhut bhi darta hai, ye* munshi *kya cheej hai* (Even ghosts fear lathis, what chance does the munshi stand)?'

Then, the Munshiji went to the collector's office and wrote in detail how he was forced to give the receipt to the unruly Yadav—due to his intimidation. The collector lodged a case of intimidation against Raiji and instructed the police to arrest him.

Next day, policemen with rifles slung across their backs reached Raiji's door. Raiji was stunned to see the well-built jawans armed with rifles. He knew that his lathi was no match for the firearms.

Raiji pleaded mildly, 'I have gotten the receipt for the taxes and I can show it to you.' He then handed over the receipt to the constable. The constable said in his stentorian voice, 'You stupid cowherd! You intimidated the tax collector and took the receipt from him. It is written on the receipt.'

The pen is mightier than the lathi.

Gods, Demons and Faith

The Priest and the Thugs

There was an old temple in Rampur village where lived a pious priest. He was engrossed in worshipping Thakurji most of the time. The village folk had the utmost faith in him. They gave him plenty of grains, jaggery, fruits, sweets and other savouries. The priest offered whatever he got to Thakurji and prayed for the well-being of the villagers.

On a hot and humid summer night, three thieves gathered in the temple's verandah and began planning a robbery. Their muffled voices reached the priest's ears, disturbing his sleep. He got up, wore his *khadau* and walked up to the thieves who were whispering into each other's ears. Their names were Kasaiya—cruel, Chalu—crafty and Bhavhin—ruthless.

Having discovered that the thieves were strategizing a theft in the village, the priest counselled them, 'Stealing someone's belongings is an act of sin. You should shun the path of sin and adopt the virtuous way of living.'

Kasaiya, Chalu and Bhavhin tried to intimidate the priest. 'Don't make noisy sermons. We will kill you if you don't stop speaking.'

But their bullying had no impact on the priest, who said:

75

Jaako rakhe sainyan
Mar sakat nahin koi
Bal na banka kar sakai
Jo jag bairi hoi

(He who is blessed with divine protection
Can be killed by none
He can't lose even a wisp of his hair
Even if the world turns against him)

Sensing that bullying wouldn't work on the priest, the thieves changed their strategy. Kasaiya argued, 'You have worshipped God for your entire life. Have you ever seen God?'

The worshipper candidly admitted that he had not seen God. Chalu then said, 'When I am stealing, I see God.' The devout hermit who had devoted his life in search of God took the thief's words to be true. 'Can I see God if I indulge in a robbery?' the priest, desperate to see God, enquired.

Chalu said, 'Yes! Why not! If I can see God, why can't you?' The priest now requested the thieves to include him in their group. Kasaiya rejected the idea, arguing, 'Why should we have a priest amidst us? He might be a burden.' Bhavhin, too, supported Kasaiya. But Chalu said, 'The priest will be a big asset. He is a seeker of God. He will never ask for a share in the booty. It will be foolish to reject such an undemanding person.'

The thieves finally decided to include the priest in their group. They asked the priest to follow them. The priest wrapped the motif of Thakurji and the conch shell in his towel and followed the thieves.

Moving slowly in the dark, the thieves reached a house and made a hole in one portion of its wall. They asked the priest to enter the house first and check if all the family members were asleep. It was a summer night. The priest saw that all the family members were sleeping on cots in the courtyard.

He came near the hole and shouted, 'Aye Kasaiya! Chalu! O Bhavhin. Everyone is in deep slumber. Come in. There is nothing to fear.'

The priest's voice woke up the house-dwellers who began yelling, *'Chor...chor* (Thief...thief)!' Hearing the voices, the thieves ran away. The priest fled too. He joined the thieves at some distance. 'Your foolishness would have cost us our lives. You are a useless fellow. Get lost,' one of the thieves shouted. But the priest apologized profusely and promised that he would not repeat his mistake. The thieves accepted his apology, and warned him against acting so foolishly ever again.

The next night, the thieves planned to steal grain from a farmer's store. The sacks of grain were stocked in a cottage near the farmer's house. Kasaiya and Chalu broke into the cottage. According to the plan, they were to balance the sacks on the heads of Bhavhin and the priest. The priest and Bhavhin were to then carry the sacks to a safe hideout.

A seasoned thief, Bhavhin lifted the sack and began moving. But the priest was unable to stand up with the grain-filled sack on his head. In an attempt to stand up with the load of sack on his head, he instinctively screamed, *'Jai Bajrang Bali* (Bravo Lord Hanuman)!' The villagers woke up and chased the thieves who somehow managed to flee. But they caught the priest.

When the villagers pounced on him, the priest pleaded, 'I was stealing so that I could catch a glimpse of God.' The priest's plea amused the villagers who soon realized that he was not a thief and that the real thieves had fled. They spared the priest.

After wandering for a few days, the priest found the thieves again and requested them to let him join them again. 'From now on, I will stay fully alert. Please pardon me and give me another chance,' the priest pleaded passionately. Bhavhin and Kasaiya thought it was too risky to keep him in their company. But Chalu reasoned with his friends once again, allowing one more chance to the priest.

On another night, the thieves broke into the house of a sweet seller. They split up to collect the booty from four different rooms. The room in which the priest entered was full of delicious sweets. The priest mused, 'While wandering with the thieves I have not made an offering to Thakurji for several days. Thakurji will be happy with these delicious sweets.'

The priest sprinkled a handful of water in a corner of the room, sanctifying it, and then sat in a lotus position to offer sweets to Thakurji. He concluded the ritual by blowing his conch shell as loudly as he could. Hearing the noise, the sweet-seller and his family members woke up and raised an alarm. The other villagers joined them and chased the thieves, who ran to save their lives. Bhavhin and Chalu bumped into a buffalo in the dark and got their limbs broken. Still, they managed to flee.

The priest did not flee. 'It will be sinful of me to run after making offerings to Thakurji. I should run only after distributing the offerings amongst the people,' he mused, asking the people to take their share of prasad. The villagers soon sensed that the priest was not a thief and let him go.

The priest again wandered for days and met the thieves again. Chalu, Kasaiya and Bhavhin were furious to see him and asked him to disappear from their sight immediately. But the priest pleaded, 'I am requesting you to keep me with you one last time. I want to see Thakurji once in my life. Kindly don't ostracize me. If I commit a mistake again, I will leave your company myself and never see you again. I am taking a vow in the name of my sacred thread to not commit a mistake and put you in trouble again.'

The thieves accepted the priest's request.

This time around, the thieves targeted a rich landlord's house. They twisted the window rods to create space and entered the house in the dead of the night. The priest entered the room in which the landlord and his wife were sleeping.

Adjacent to the landlord's room was the kitchen, stocked with milk, sugar and fine rice. The priest thought of preparing kheer and offering the same to Thakurji. The priest lit the stove carefully and cooked the kheer. He offered it to Thakurji. Then, he saw the landlord's wife's sleeping on the bed; her palm was wide open.

'The offering to Thakurji is incomplete without distributing it amongst others,' the priest mused. When he saw the open palm of the landlord's sleeping wife, he spooned out the kheer—still hot—from the pot and placed it on the woman's palm.

The hot kheer woke the woman and she screamed in pain. The others in the family rushed to help her. The thieves ran as soon as they heard her scream. The priest did not run, and the family members sensed that he was not a thief and let him go.

But the priest was very sad now. He was upset that he could not see God despite resorting to thievery. Out of disgust, he decided to jump into the temple's well to end his life. 'O God! I have failed to see a glimpse of you. Now, I am ending my life's journey,' the priest ranted in a fit of depression and jumped into the well.

Thakurji, with a halo on his head, descended, saving the priest. 'Lo and behold! I am here with you,' Thakurji said. The priest burst into tears. He had finally seen God for whom he had been searching his entire life.

You will find God if you are truly devoted to Him.

The Young Boy and Hanumanji

Girdhari Choubey was a priest in Lord Hanuman's temple located in Tandawa village. He was a devout worshipper who prayed to Hanumanji every morning and evening. He would never eat his meal without offering a laddu—known to be a favourite of Hanumanji—to the Lord's idol. He prepared the offerings with the help of his teenage son who lived with him.

The priest and his son lived on the charity of the villagers. One day, the priest was supposed to go to another village for some important work. He was required to have an overnight stay in that village and return next morning. It would be too late to make the offering by the time he returned next day.

So, he bought five laddus from the local confectionary and gave them to his son. He instructed him, 'Offer two laddus to Hanumanji and keep three for yourself.' The priest then proceeded with his evening ritual, explaining to his son exactly what was required for the next morning.

Before leaving, the priest was unsure if his son would carry out the rituals properly. He feared that naïve as he was, he would eat all the laddus, inviting the wrath of Hanumanji.

He had seldom given the responsibility of performing the rituals to his son so far. Moreover, the boy was too young to worship in the desired manner. But the trip was urgent and the priest could not avoid it. He left the temple in a pensive mood, hoping that his son would carry out the required chore.

As dawn broke, the boy got up, took a bath and put two laddus in a bowl. Then he bowed before Hanumanji and placed the offerings near his feet. He asked Hanumanji to eat the offerings. He left the place and shut the door of the temple so that Hanumanji could eat in peace.

After some time, the boy opened the door to find the two laddus he had offered lying uneaten in the bowl. He was hungry and desperately wanted to eat his share. 'But how can I eat before Hanumanji eats his share? My father has asked me to feed Hanumanji first,' the boy mused. He once again prayed to Hanumanji, asking him to eat the laddus, and shut the door.

After a few minutes, he opened the door again to find that laddus were still lying uneaten. Hungry as he was, he got furious. He now added one more laddu in the bowl and whipped out a baton, shouting at the Lord, 'You have kept me hungry for a long time now. I have spared one laddu from my share, and I am keeping only two for myself. If you still don't eat, I will smash you with this baton. Hurry up and gulp down the three laddus quickly.' The boy screamed at the idol and shut the door again in a huff.

After a while, he opened the door and saw that all the three laddus had vanished from the bowl. He was ecstatic and ate the two laddus that were left for him. Then, he began playing with the other children.

Later, the priest arrived and anxiously enquired if the boy had performed the rituals and made the offering. 'Yes, I offered three laddus to Hanumanji. He ate them all. I ate only two laddus,' the boy said promptly. The priest thought his son was lying; how could Hanumanji eat the offering made to him? He lost his cool at his son's 'mischief' and gave him a tight slap.

The son was puzzled. 'Why did you beat me? I first offered two laddus to Hanumanji, just like you had suggested. But he did not eat them. Then, I spared one more from my share for him. This time, Hanumanji ate all the three laddus. I was left with only two laddus which I ate later. Now, instead of compensating me with a laddu, you have slapped me,' the boy said, weeping.

Equally perplexed, the priest then decided to test his son. 'I want to see with my own eyes if Hanumanji eats the laddus offered by you.' The boy got ready and asked his father, 'Give me three laddus. Hanumanji does not eat less than three. He didn't eat them when I gave him two.'

As the sun set, the priest prepared the laddus and gave them to his son, asking him to feed Hanumanji. Now, the boy, holding a baton in his hand, placed the three laddus near the Lord's feet and warned, 'You ate one of my laddus. Yet, my father slapped me. Now, if you don't eat the laddus I am offering, my father will beat me more. In that case, I will smash your head.'

Then, the boy came out and shut the door. After some time, he asked his father to open the door. The priest opened the door, and to his pleasant surprise, he saw that all the three laddus had vanished from the bowl.

Children are innocent; God doesn't mind their pranks.

The Skull and Raghobaba

There lived a priest named Raghobaba in a village called Govindpur. He enjoyed widespread fame for his knowledge about the divine scriptures, Vedas and Upanishads. He practised occult and black magic as well. On top of all that, he was also a fortune teller who could tell the past, present and future of his followers by reading their foreheads. The villagers unwaveringly believed in Raghobaba's supernatural abilities.

While wandering near the village one day, Raghobaba saw a human skull lying abandoned in a maze of bushes along the path. He picked up the skull and observed it minutely. He saw that the skull contained a hidden message: 'I have suffered many torrid spells in proportion to my karma in my worldly life. But I am still left with some share of sufferings to undergo.'

The priest was bewildered to read the message. 'It is an old skull. The man who wore it must have died long ago. He must have undergone all the rituals of his worldly existence and died. This skull is as good as a lifeless stone. But why does it say that it is still left with some share of sufferings to undergo? What else does the skull have to suffer?' the priest mused.

He contemplated for a while but failed to figure out the

83

meaning of the message. Pondering over the karma and destiny of the man whose skull it was, Raghobaba kept it in his bag and reached home by the time the sun had set. He kept the skull at the place of worship in his home.

Next morning, the priest's wife got up to begin her household chores. She picked up the broom to mop the place of worship. But when she saw the skull lying there, she got furious. 'My husband has turned senile due to his advancing age. Why would he place a skull at the place of worship?' she thought and then reprimanded Raghobaba.

'We already have the statues of Lord Shiva and Goddess Kali! You have placed a skull—an unholy object—among the Gods and Goddesses. Are you in your senses?' the woman screamed.

The priest calmly said, 'It is not an ordinary skull. It carries a message which I am trying to figure out. I am working on unravelling the mystery of the skull.' The woman fell silent to avoid a quarrel with her husband. But she was not convinced by the priest's logic.

Raghobaba took a bath and sat at his place of worship, chanting the mantras from the Vedas and Upanishads. He offered flowers and put turmeric paste on the skull kept amongst the statues of other Gods and Goddesses. His wife's blood boiled but she maintained her composure.

As it happened, one day, the priest went out. The woman crushed the skull with a pestle and threw its powdery remains on a pile of waste outside her home. When the priest returned, he did not find the skull at its designated place. He enquired his wife about it.

The woman shot back, 'I crushed it and threw it out of the house. Lord Shiva and Goddess Kali live in our home. The Gods have blessed us with children. It was strange to have a skull at our place of worship. Graveyards and cremation grounds are the right places for a skull.'

But Raghobaba did not lose his temper at all. He smiled and told his wife, 'Your act has helped me figure out the subtle message contained in the skull. The owner of the skull had died long ago. But the skull was still left with his share of suffering. By getting crushed and converted into powder the skull is now done with what he was supposed to undergo in this world.'

The woman, too, calmed down. She realized that her husband was not as strange as she had thought he was. Rather, he was a pursuer of knowledge in the philosophy of karma and destiny.

One faces one's karma even after one's death.

GODS, DEMONS AND FAITH

The Rakshasi's Sacrifice

Once upon a time there lived a king with his seven sons who were brave and handsome, and loved each other. They were fond of hunting. They hunted birds and animals to feast on with their parents and courtiers every day.

Once, the seven brothers, chasing a deer, strayed into a deep forest. While the deer vanished into the dense woods, the princes entered the area ruled by seven rakshasi sisters. The rakshasis captured the princes and claimed one prince each, according to their age. The eldest rakshasi got the eldest prince as her share. Similarly, the youngest rakshasi got the youngest prince.

The demon sisters agreed to make love to their respective princes. They collectively decided to kill and feast on the princes once they had satisfied their sexual desires. The princes, despite their physical prowess, found it hard to cope with the rakshasis' lust. But it saved them from dying; so they kept at it.

As the days passed, the youngest rakshasi fell in love with her prince. She gave up the idea of eating him. She treated him as her husband and cared for him well. The prince, too, showed his fondness for the youngest rakshasi who massaged his feet before going to sleep and offered him delicious fruits and meat to eat.

One day, the rakshashis had a meeting to announce that they had fully satiated their desire with the princes and the time to kill them and feast on them had come. They decided to kill their princes the next evening, when they returned after their chores in the forest. But they didn't communicate this decision to the princes in their custody.

The youngest rakshasi attended the meeting but stayed silent throughout. She was opposed to the idea of killing the man she had fallen in love with. She began thinking of some way to save her man.

As she went to bed, she began massaging the prince's feet. But she started sobbing. Her teardrops fell on the prince. 'Why are you weeping?' the prince asked.

The rakshasi revealed the plan to the prince. 'I am weeping because I will turn into a widow tomorrow evening. My sisters will kill and devour all of you.'

The prince got frightened and asked, 'Is there a way we can save our lives?'

To this, the rakshasi suggested, 'Early morning tomorrow, I will open the back door, which leads to the stable. You will find seven horses tied in the stable. Alert your brothers about my sisters' conspiracy. You all should silently sneak out of the house once we leave the place. Ride the horses and run away.'

The youngest prince shared the idea with his brothers the next morning after the rakshasis had left the house. The youngest rakshasi had opened the back door. The princes found the horses and fled.

That day, the rakshashis did not enjoy their outing for too long and returned early, only to find that the princes had fled. Soon, they regrouped and began searching for the princes. In a short while, the rakshasis got very close to the princes on horseback.

One of the sisters caught hold of the tail of the horse that carried the youngest prince. The youngest rakshashi shouted, 'O sister! Stay alert. The prince might cut the tail which will be left in your hands and then the horse will gallop away.' The youngest prince got the hint; whipping out his sword, he cut off the tail. Taking a cue from their youngest brother, the others too chopped their horses' tails which the other six rakshashis were holding on to.

This way, the princes managed to get out of the borders of the rakshasis' kingdom and soon entered their own. The rakshasis were trapped in their own kingdoms, and so could not follow them out of their territory. Stuck, the eldest rakshasi asked, 'Now that you all are out of our reach, tell us who helped you escape?'

The youngest prince told the sisters that it was the youngest rakshasi who had shown them the way. The six rakshasis were furious with their youngest sister for betraying them. They killed her and devoured her to avenge the loss of the princes.

Some demons can have better qualities than human beings.

The Elephant and the Worms

There lived a fisherman on the banks of River Saryu. Every morning, he would take his boat to the river and return with plenty of fish trapped in his net in the evening. Breakfast, lunch or dinner—he ate fish for all his meals.

The only skills he had were rowing and fishing. His world was confined to his boat, river, net and fish. He would stay engrossed in untangling his net even when he was at home, away from the river and his boat. When he slept, he would dream of fish and the river. As soon as he got up, he would go to his boat, anchored on the riverbank.

In between his routine centred on the river and the boat, he would briefly talk to his wife and children. He was a content man. He would bring home enough fish for the entire family and he would also sell them for adequate money to meet their daily needs. His wife didn't expect much from her husband.

When he grew old, he died in peace.

He was born as an elephant in a deep forest in his next life. His size grew enormous and he became robust, feasting on the rich fodder in the woods. He moved in herds with other elephants in search of food and water.

Once, the forest was struck by a long spell of drought. The sun was harsh and powerful. Most of the streams dried up in the face of the blazing sun. The animals in the forest wandered here and there in search of water. The elephant, too, was roaming around with his herd when he spotted a stream in between rocks.

The elephant who had been a fisherman in his previous life drove his trunk through the zigzagged rocks and sucked on the water in the crevices to quench his thirst. But he was unable to pull his trunk out after he was done drinking. His trunk was trapped in the rocks. He didn't know how to take it out and rejoin his herd.

The members of his herd tried to rescue him. They camped there for a couple of days in the hope that their peer would free himself and they would move on together. But eventually, they gave up and moved on, leaving him alone.

Struggling to get his trunk out, the elephant rubbed his neck on the rocks. His neck got wounded and started bleeding. Soon, several worms attached themselves to the wound which began festering. His pain grew as the worms ate into him. Unable to bear the excruciating pain, he let out a trumpet that cut through the air.

Lord Shiva and Goddess Parvati were passing by the spot where the elephant was howling in pain. The Goddess's eyes fell on the animal in distress and she asked Shiva to rescue him.

Shiva said, 'It is a mortal world. Any creature that is born is destined to die. And every creature gets the fruit of his karma. The elephant is suffering on account of what he did in his previous life.'

'But what could an elephant have done to suffer such pain? He lives on leaves and water. He is born into a breed that is not carnivorous. I am sure he never perpetrated violence on other animals, like tigers and lions do. Countless worms are feasting on him, aggravating his pain. How has the elephant harmed the worms?' Parvati argued, goading Shiva to help the animal.

Shiva said, 'The elephant was a fisherman in his previous birth. He feasted on countless fish. Those fish have been born as worms in this birth. Now, the fish are doing to him what he did to them. We are not supposed to interfere with the order of nature. Forget about the elephant and move on.'

But overwhelmed by pity, Parvati entreated to Shiva, 'My Lord! It is hard for me to move on, leaving the animal in distress. I won't move unless you help the elephant.' Parvati was rigid about her demand.

Shiva then went to the elephant and 'blessed' him to die immediately. The elephant died. Shiva told Parvati, 'I have done the best that I could for the elephant. His liberation lay in his death. Now that he is dead, his pain has vanished. Now, he will be born as another creature and will lead his life's journey according to the karma he has performed in his life as an elephant,' Shiva said.

Goddess Parvati was satisfied and moved on with Shiva thereafter.

You always have to pay for what you have done in your previous life; the cycle of life and rebirth continues.

GODS, DEMONS AND FAITH

The Brahmin and the Washerwoman

Once a Brahmin priest, Gangadhar, lived with his son, Raghav, in a certain village. The priest would perform religious rituals for a living. His job barely fetched him two meals a day. The father-son duo lived in immense hardship.

The Brahmin discouraged his son from priesthood. He got Raghav educated and advised him to go out in the city to get a job. Raghav followed his father's advice for he had seen how hard it was to sustain life as a priest.

Gangadhar decided on an 'auspicious' day to send off his son. Raghav, after touching his father's feet and receiving his blessings, left for the city in search of a job. After travelling some distance, he entered a forest which had a hut and an old woman tying pieces of string in pairs.

Seeing that the old woman was doing something unusual, Raghav stopped and asked her, 'What are you doing? What is the use of pairing the pieces of strings?' The woman said, 'I have supernatural skills. The scattered strings symbolize brides and grooms. I am making pairs the brides and grooms.'

Getting inquisitive, Raghav asked, 'Can you tell me who my wife will be?' The old woman pulled out a string which she said represented Raghav. She picked up another string and observed it carefully. Then she entwined it with the one which was Raghav and announced, 'You will have a *dhoban* girl as your wife.'

Raghav got anxious. He was a Brahmin. He couldn't have a dhoban for a wife. He asked the old woman, 'How can I have a dhoban for a wife? I am a Brahmin. You know that a Brahmin can't marry a dhoban.'

The old woman said, 'It is what destiny has in store for you. Lord Brahma has already sent a dhoban girl to marry you in this world. I have simply have identified her.' Raghav asked her about the dhoban's whereabouts and the old woman obliged him with the information.

Raghav travelled across the village and identified the house that the old woman had indicated. He knocked on the door. A pretty girl came out to enquire about what he was looking for. Raghav guessed that the girl was his future spouse. He asked her about her parents. The girl told him that they were off washing clothes on the riverbank. Raghav told the girl that he had something important to discuss with her parents and asked her to escort him to them. The girl was naive. She readily agreed. On the way, Raghav was in a dilemma. He thought of killing the girl. 'I will kill her. If she dies I will save myself from marrying this lowly woman. I must prove the old woman wrong to keep the honour of my divine caste,' Raghav mused while travelling.

They were passing a desolate patch on their way to the river where the girl's parents were washing clothes. Raghav whipped out a knife and slashed her throat from behind. The girl fell to the ground, bleeding. He threw her body in the pond and decamped. Assuming that the girl had died, Raghav returned to his village. He made an excuse of not feeling well

GODS, DEMONS AND FAITH

and promised his father he would hunt for a job as soon as he was well again.

A Brahmin from another village went to take a dip in the pond in which Raghav had thrown the girl. The Brahmin saw the girl floating on the surface and rescued her. She was alive but grievously wounded. The Brahmin brought her home. He and his wife got the girl treated by a vaidya. She recovered and began living with the Brahmin couple.

The couple did not have children. The man and his wife developed affection for the girl and accepted her as a 'blessing' from Mother Ganga. The girl too began treating the couple as her parents and grew under their loving care.

When the girl attained the marriageable age, the Brahmin began looking for a suitable groom for her. He came to know about Raghav through certain contacts and acquaintances in Gangadhar's village. Subsequently, he went to Gangadhar and proposed his daughter's marriage to Raghav. Gangadhar found the guest's proposal quite suitable and agreed to marry his son to the latter's daughter. Raghav and the girl were tied in nuptial knots on an auspicious day amidst chants of the Vedic mantras and benedictions. Raghav was happy to get a beautiful wife. He was convinced that he had proven the old woman wrong who had predicted that he would marry a dhoban girl.

Once, Raghav, in a jolly mood, took his newly-wed wife to the forest in which the old woman lived and boasted how he had proved her prophecy wrong. 'I have married a Brahmin girl. Your prediction has gone wrong in our case,' he announced before the old woman. The old woman smiled, and said, 'Look at her neck. There is the mark of the wound caused by your knife. She is the same girl you had attacked and thrown into a pond.'

Raghav looked at his wife's neck. The girl confirmed how

she had gotten the cut mark on her neck. Then he surrendered before the old woman, touching her feet. He got his wife to touch the woman's feet and seek blessing for a happy conjugal life. The old woman announced, 'I have done nothing on my own. Lord Brahma—the God of Destiny—had ordained you to marry this girl. I just informed you in advance what destiny had in store for you. Now, you should live in a loving relationship as husband and wife.'

Thereafter, the couple lived merrily.

It is wrong to kill someone, no matter what the reason. We cannot ignore the sin committed by the man to make sure that the prophecy didn't come true.

GODS, DEMONS AND FAITH

Pranks, Intrigues,
Struggle and Entertainment

The Scholar and His 'Heavenly' Beard

There was a priest named Scholar in a certain village. The king had immense respect for him. The king trusted him with all sorts of rituals in the palace. He had the utmost faith in Scholar and believed that the priest could ward off any trouble that afflicted his kingdom by the power of his prayers.

The king's adoration for Scholar made other courtiers envious. Some jealous courtiers conspired to end Scholar's access to the king. One day, a courtier told the king, 'It is a very auspicious day. If you get a strand of Scholar's beard on this day, you will surely go to heaven.'

The king found the courtier's proposal harmless. Agreeing to it, he sent his emissary to bring the priest to the palace with all respect. When the priest entered, the king entreated, 'Learned priest! I have to ask you for something.'

'I will put my head on the line for you. Tell me what you want, My Lord.'

'Nothing precious! Part with a strand of your beard for me.'

The priest, who had a flowing beard and hair on his head,

instantly plucked a strand of his beard and passed it on to the king.

Then, a minister asked for another strand of beard from Scholar. The benign priest obliged the minister too, giving him a strand of his beard. When the priest took leave from the king, he found another courtier making the same demand. The priest obliged him too.

But when the priest came out of the king's room, he saw a deluge of people scrambling outside to get a strand of his beard. The report that the possession of the priest's beard was a ticket to heaven had spread like wildfire in the entire kingdom.

The crowd jumped on the priest ruthlessly, plucking at his beard. The priest began screaming in pain and somehow fled from the melee. His face was swollen and blood was oozing from it. The crowd had also uprooted the hair on his head. There were bloody bald patches all over his head. Yelling in pain, the priest ran like a madman. People followed him in the hundreds.

In the meantime, a village boy had just returned home after cutting grass for his cattle. His old and infirm mother was at home. As soon as she saw her son, the old woman screamed, 'O my doomed son! Where were you? All the villagers have gotten Scholar's whisker, which will lead them straight to heaven. Only we are left without the whisker.'

'What should I do now?' the bewildered son asked his mother. The mother shouted back, 'You fool! You are still clueless. Run fast to catch the priest and get a strand of his hair.'

The boy, who was still holding the sickle in his hand, ran, catching hold of the priest. He could not find a single whisker either on his face or on his head. In a hurry, he slashed a part of the priest's cheek so that he could search for a whisker in peace at home.

THE GREATEST FOLK TALES OF BIHAR

It is not known if the king and the villagers who had taken the priest's hair went to heaven. But the priest departed for his heavenly abode even before he reached his home.

Beware of cunning people.

The Malpua Tale

Malpua has been the most sought-after delicacy in the rural homes of the Gangetic plains for centuries. The first item that a bride cooks after coming to her in-laws' home is malpua. No major festival can be celebrated without it. Holi, Chhat or Ramnavami—malpua is a compulsory dish in all cultural and religious carnivals.

But poor cultivators rarely get to cook and eat it. It involves costly ingredients—a fine variety of wheat flour, milk, sugar, ghee and dry fruits. The landless farmhands struggle hard to even manage two meals of coarse grain a day and are largely dependent on their high-caste *maliks* to get malpuas on special occasions.

Ramraj and his wife Dhania were landless farm workers living in a certain village. They lived in poverty but loved each other. The woman affectionately cooked whatever Ramraj brought home after his day's work at the landowner's farm. She would always give more to her husband than she would keep for herself.

One day, Ramraj felt a strong urge to eat malpua. 'We could not eat malpua last Holi because our malik's father had passed away and he did not celebrate the festival. I feel like eating malpua now,' Ramraj told his wife. Dhania entreated, 'Get the sugar, milk, ghee and wheat flour. I will arrange for some dry fruits from our master's home and will cook it. I know how to prepare mouthwatering malpuas.'

Ramraj worked hard and for longer hours that day, earning relatively more. He bought the ingredients for malpua and handed them over to his wife. But the woman could manage to prepare only five malpuas out of the flour, ghee, sugar and milk that Ramraj had brought home. Now, a dispute arose between the couple over sharing the malpuas, which were present in an odd number.

'Please let me have three malpuas and keep two for yourself,' Ramraj told his wife.

The wife, who always gave more to Ramraj, was unwilling to part with more when it came to the mouthwatering malpuas—a rare delicacy she had cooked years after her wedding with Ramraj. 'I rounded the dough, sat before the oven in the heat. I arranged for the dry fruits. I should get three malpuas for my share,' Dhania argued. Ramraj retorted, 'Had I not brought the flour, sugar and ghee, how would you have cooked it? I toiled hard in the field to earn the money to buy these ingredients. Moreover, I was the one who proposed the idea of making malpuas to you. You should behave like an obedient wife and give me more malpuas.'

The argument between the husband and wife snowballed into a fierce quarrel. While the delicacy was getting cold and losing its flavour, Ramraj and Dhania got locked in a cantankerous duel. When Ramraj yelled, 'I should get more malpuas!' his wife cried, 'I should get more!' The longing for malpuas had snuffed out the love between Ramraj and Dhania.

Quarrelling for hours, the couple reached an agreement.

They decided to not speak to each other, with the precondition that the one who spoke first would lose, getting only two malpuas for his/her share. The victor—the one who didn't speak first—would automatically get three in his/her share, as per the agreement.

Ramraj and Dhania fell silent after the protracted bout of squabbling. Darkness enveloped the surroundings. The neighbours and other villagers had fallen asleep long ago. The man and woman went to bed with empty stomachs. The malpuas—prepared with so much care—lay uncared for.

The neighbours saw Ramraj's door shut at the break of dawn. But as the sun rose and the day advanced, they got suspicious. They called other villagers to find out why Ramraj and Dhania had not opened the door even when noon was nearing. The villagers knocked on Ramraj's door, repeatedly asking him to open it.

Their suspicions grew when the couple did not respond to their frantic calls. The villagers finally broke the door open and barged inside to find both Ramraj and his wife lying in their respective beds as if they were dead.

The villagers shouted at the top of their voices but neither Ramraj nor Dhania budged. They finally concluded that the husband and wife had died and began preparing to cremate them at the nearby cremation ground.

The villagers arranged for a pyre each for the husband and wife. They put Ramraj and Dhania on the two pyres kept side by side. Then, they divided themselves into two groups made up of four persons each and lifted the pyres on their shoulders.

In the meantime, Ramraj yelled, 'O stupid woman. I accept my defeat by speaking first. I do not want to get cremated just for the sake of eating three malpuas.'

The wife, too, got out of the pyre. Both the husband and wife ate the malpuas that had been prepared nearly sixteen hours ago. They had become cold and tasteless. The villagers were stunned at the couple's stupidity.

Poverty breeds pettiness.

Andher Nagari, Chowpat Raja
(The Dark City and the Whimsical King)

Once upon a time, there was a city called Andher Nagri. Literally translated, the name meant 'dark city'. The king of Andher Nagri was a man of whims and fancies. He had decreed that everything was to be sold at the same price. Thus, a sweetmeat cost as much as a lump of salt. Meat had the same price as spinach. Be it potatoes or luscious mangoes—they cost one paisa each. Whether it was a fine variety of rice or coarse grain—every edible item was available at throwaway prices.

One fine day, a hermit and his disciple visited Andher Nagri, where they saw a taxman shouting at a pumpkin vendor waiting for customers in the marketplace. 'You are supposed to give me at least seven pumpkins as tax. But you have brought only six pumpkins,' the tax collector barked at the vendor.

Without waiting for the vendor to respond, the fuming collector lifted all the six pumpkins along with the basket in which they were kept. 'I am taking away your basket. It will compensate for the seventh pumpkin,' the taxman shouted and moved to another shop.

Feeling helpless and harried, the vendor approached the king and narrated his plight. The king fumed, 'You should have brought seven pumpkins. You had only six. Now, you have come to complain against the tax-collector who was only carrying out his official duty.' The king ordered his guards to whip the vendor as punishment. Bruised and battered, the vendor left the palace.

Disturbed to see all this, the hermit's disciple advised him to leave Andher Nagri at once. 'It is a dangerous place, my master. There is no justice here. We should go somewhere else,' the disciple said.

But the hermit did not agree. 'Things are available at a cheap price in this city. Why should we move elsewhere?' the hermit argued.

The disciple thought otherwise. 'You may live here if you so wish. But I am going to live somewhere else. If you ever land in any trouble, do let me know,' the disciple said, taking leave of the hermit.

The hermit began living under a banyan tree in Andher Nagri. Days turned into weeks and weeks into months.

One day, thieves broke into a trader's house, and a portion of its mud wall caved in, killing a thief. Learning of her husband's death, the thief's wife rushed to the king's court. 'Who will feed me and my children now, my Lord? My husband died in the middle of a theft at the trader's house.'

The king ordered his guards to arrest the trader and bring him to the court. Handcuffed, the trader was produced before the king. 'Why did you build such a dilapidated house? Its wall collapsed, and the thief was crushed under the debris. Who will feed the thief's wife and children now?'

The trader fell at the king's feet and pleaded, 'My Lord! It was not my fault. The mason used substandard material to construct the wall. He should be punished instead.'

The king saw reason in this. He spared the trader and ordered that the mason be arrested. His guards arrested the mason, but he also pleaded innocent. 'A prostitute is to be blamed, my Lord. She was passing by while I was building that wall and the sight of her distracted me. As a result, I could not concentrate on making a strong wall.'

The king ordered the guards to arrest the prostitute. When produced before the king, the prostitute, too, begged for mercy. 'My Lord, I haven't committed any offence. I was on my way to meet my paramour. I did nothing to distract the worker,' she said in her defence.

The king soon had the prostitute's paramour arrested. He did not allow the 'accused' to defend himself and ordered that he be hanged to death. But the hangman found his neck too thin to fit into the noose. The king was informed.

'You stupid man! You don't have common sense. Substitute the guilty with a fat man whose neck can fit the noose and hang him. Simple!' the king shouted at the hangman.

And lo and behold! The guards spotted the plump hermit and decided that he was a proper substitute. Faced with a death sentence, a frightened hermit sought time to offer his final prayers. The king obliged him.

The hermit in distress sent a message to his disciple. The latter rushed to the hermit's aid and devised a plan to save him. 'Let's go to the king and start scrambling over wearing the noose,' he told the hermit. The latter had confidence in his disciple's wisdom. He agreed.

The duo reached the king's palace. When the king signalled the hangman to hang the hermit, the disciple came forward and offered his neck instead. The hermit protested, 'The king has ordered me to wear the noose. So I should be hanged.'

This argument between the hermit and the hermit's disciple continued for a while.

A little perplexed, the king remarked, 'I have seen people struggle for survival, but you guys are strange! Why are both of you vying to die?'

The disciple politely said, 'My Lord, it's an auspicious moment. Anyone who dies right now will become the king of the three worlds—the earth, the sky and the sea.'

The king was not only foolish but he was also greedy. He instantly drove away the saint and his disciple and got himself hanged to death.

Foolish and whimsical people are always doomed.

PRANKS, INTRIGUES, STRUGGLE AND ENTERTAINMENT

The Sinner and the Khaini

There lived a young woman in a certain village. She could not see, hear, or speak because she was blind, deaf and dumb. She lived in a ramshackle hut in the corner of the village. She worked in fields and earned just enough to sustain herself.

Her parents had died long ago. She had no siblings. No one would offer to marry her. She had led a neglected existence. But the farmers of the village employed her in their farms, enabling her to carry on with her life. Some elderly women, at times, got her to massage their bodies, offering her food and used clothes.

On a rainy night, when most of the residents were indoors, a village youth broke into her hut and forced himself on her. Early the next morning, an agriculturist went near her hut to ask her to assist him in his field. But he noticed that she was wounded and her clothes were torn. Unable to speak and explain, she was sobbing and beating her chest wildly.

As he saw her haggard look, the agriculturist soon sensed what had happened to the woman. He congregated the elders of the village to show them her plight. The village panchayat decided to donate food and clothes to the victim till she recovered, and set up a two-man committee of investigators to search for the culprit who had committed this ghastly sin on the helpless woman.

The investigators were reputed for their integrity and commitment to social cause. But it was hard for them to identify the sinner as the victim could neither have identified her tormentor nor could have spoken to explain his features.

After a few days, one of the investigators—always on the lookout for the sinner—saw a youth picking up bits of khaini littered on a pathway. Someone had spit out the remains after chewing it. The youth was gathering and piecing together the thrown pieces of khaini strewn there. He rubbed the bits of khaini with lime and kept it between his teeth and lips.

The investigator, who was watching the repulsive act of eating the chewed bits of khaini, had the intuition that the same youth might have attacked the woman. 'Only a person who can undertake this abominable act of eating chewed and thrown khaini can attack a helpless woman,' he guessed and soon caught hold of the youth, presenting him to the panchayat. The second investigator, too, approved his colleague's action.

To be sure of the youth's offence, the panchayat elders began beating and questioning him. The youth eventually confessed that he had forced himself on the woman. The panchayat members tonsured the youth's head and made him ride on a donkey's back across the village as punishment.

Sinners cannot hide their sin for long.

PRANKS, INTRIGUES, STRUGGLE AND ENTERTAINMENT

The Leaf and the Lump

There lived a lump of earth a big and round leaf of a Pipal tree together in a field. They were inseparable and they didn't live apart even for a moment. Day or night, lived together, enjoying each other's company.

Others got jealous of their friendship. The storm and rain conspired to end the bond between the two. The storm decided to sweep the leaf away to a distant land while the rain resolved to dissolve the lump, ending its existence.

The lump and the leaf got a whiff of the conspiracy between the rain and the storm and tried to think of ways to ward off the danger.

As per their plan, the rain struck first. The lump broke into wails, telling the leaf, 'O dear! Our long friendship is about to end now. The torrent is dissolving me fast. Unable to bear the pounding, I am about to dissolve into the mud soon.'

The leaf smiled and said, 'I will not let you die as long as I am around.' Then, he jumped and sat atop the lump, canopying his friend against the rain. After some time, the rain stopped and the lump survived.

Now came the storm's turn. It carried the leaf with itself.

Frightened, the leaf cried, 'O brother lump! It is hard for me to hold on. I am losing my balance as the storm is trying to take me away from you.'

'Nothing to be worried about, I won't let you go as long as I am alive,' the lump said and sat on the leaf.

The storm, too, passed. The lump and leaf, having survived, shared smiles. Their bond of friendship and their will to use their strength to protect each other had helped them survive rain and storm.

Thereafter, they lived merrily.

Friends in need are friends indeed.

PRANKS, INTRIGUES, STRUGGLE AND ENTERTAINMENT

Ulua, Bulua and I

We were three friends: Ulua, Bulua and I. We lived and played together all the time. We would go out to catch fish in the pond and play *guili-danda*, kabaddi, *haal* and *luka-chhipi* on the village streets.

On a cloudy day, Ulua proposed that we go fishing. Bulua and I agreed, and we set out to catch fish in the pond, fyke nets in our hands. Ulua caught a *garai*, a small and round fish, Bulua caught a rohu, a bigger fish, and I caught a crab.

We assembled, each with our catch. Ulua lit a bonfire. We dropped our catches into the fire. Ulua's garai and Bulua's rohu got roasted well. My crab got burnt to ashes.

Ulua consoled me, saying that there was nothing to be sad about and gave me a piece of his roasted garai. Bulua gave me a part of his roasted rohu. All of us ate together and went back to the pond to drink water and wash the layer of mud off us.

Ulua and Bulua bathed and drank water. A poor swimmer, I got stuck and was about to drown. Soon, Ulua and Bulua jumped into the pond. Ulua held me by my hands and Bullua by my legs and pulled me out.

Then, we went to play kabaddi and luka-chhipi.

Live in the spirit of cooperation.

The Badshah and His Youngest Daughter

Once upon a time, there lived a *badshah*. He had seven daughters. Once, the badshah asked his daughters, 'Whom would you give credit to for your fortunate life?' Six of his daughters told him they owed their fortune and happiness to him.

But his youngest daughter, Yashmin, said that whatever she had was because of her destiny. The king got angry with her and exiled her to a forest with a maid to test the power of her destiny. Overwhelmed by pity, her mother concealed a precious stone in her hair and advised her to use it when she felt the need.

The young princess and the maid began living a miserable life in the shade of a tree in the forest. The princess, who was used to bathing in rose water in the royal chamber, now had to go without bathing for days in the open surroundings. One day, the maid got a makeshift hut of palm leaves erected to ensure privacy and brought water from the nearby stream so that the princess could bathe. Yashmin took a bath after many days in the forest.

The princess excelled at making attractive designs on

115

handkerchiefs and pillow covers. But she didn't have cotton, needle or string to try her skill. One day, she handed to the maid the precious stone that her mother had given her, asking the latter to sell it off and buy the materials needed for making handkerchiefs and pillow covers.

The obedient maid bought clothes, needles and strings by selling the stone in the market. The princess then made attractive handkerchiefs and pillow covers, and the maid sold them, fetching money to fulfil their basic needs. After the princess accumulated some money, she decided to get a mud house built for more privacy. She engaged a labourer to dig the foundation for a small mud house near the place she was living in.

The labourer worked very hard with his spade but failed to cut the rocky and hard earth. The princess noticed that there was something hard on the surface, preventing the spade from breaking into it. She inspected the spot and found that a brick of gold was embedded just below the surface. She asked the labourer to leave and dug out the brick. Then, she asked her maid to sell it in the market. The maid brought a bagful of cash in exchange for the brick of gold.

Now, Yashmin had enough money to build a decent house to live in. She employed masons to build a house better than her father's. The masons built a magnificent mansion. She started leading a luxurious life in the mansion. Meanwhile, her family members were completely unaware of the change in her fortunes.

One day, her father thought of going on a pilgrimage and asked his six daughters what they wanted as gifts from him. The six daughters enthusiastically asked for their desired things. Then he remembered his youngest daughter and asked a maid to call on her to find out what she needed.

Yashmin conveyed through the maid that she needed a *haruni pankha* to cool herself in the harsh forest weather. Her father included Yashmin's wish amongst those of the others and proceeded for the pilgrimage.

After offering prayers at the pilgrimage, the badshah bought all the items that his daughters had asked for. But he failed to find the fan despite searching for it everywhere. The badshah didn't want to disappoint his daughter who was living away from him. Someone told him that Harun Rashid—the king of the holy city—possessed the fan he was looking for.

The badshah went to Harun Rashid's palace, seeking the fan. Harun Rashid was reluctant to part with his special fan but thought it improper to rebuff a fellow king. He gifted the fan to the guest.

The badshah offered to pay munificently for it but the latter pleaded, 'It is inappropriate for me to sell my fan to a fellow king. I am gifting it to you in your honour.'

The badshah returned with the gifts to his kingdom. He sent the fan via a maid to Yashmin. The maid, seeing that the princess was busy praying, dropped the fan in her room through a window and departed.

After some time, her maid saw the fan and gave it to the princess. Yashmin whirled the fan, feeling refreshed in its aromatic air. Incidentally, she whirled it in the reverse direction and Harun Rashid suddenly appeared. 'Who are you?' the princess asked. Harun Rashid introduced himself, telling her that it was a magical fan that he had gifted to her father and whenever she would whirl it in reverse gear, he would appear.

Now, Yashmin would whirl the fan in the reverse direction whenever she wanted to meet Harun Rashid, who was smart and handsome. Gradually, Yashmin and Harun Rashid fell in

PRANKS, INTRIGUES, STRUGGLE AND ENTERTAINMENT

love. One day, Harun Rashid proposed to marry the princess. Yashmin happily agreed.

Harun Rashid got red carpets rolled out between Yashmin's mansion and her father's palace. After tying the nuptial knot, both the princess and her groom approached the badshah to seek his blessings. Yashmin asked him, 'Now tell me, whom should I attribute my fortune to?' Her father felt ashamed and expressed genuine happiness on seeing his daughter.

You will always have your way if you are industrious and have luck favouring you.

The Shyamkaran Horse

Once there lived a king named Mahipal. He had three sons. The first son was called Jay. The second was Vijay and the third was Mahir.

The king asked them their interests when they grew up and sent them to their chosen centres of learning. The boys went to different places to acquire knowledge in their preferred fields. Jay, Vijay and Mahir returned home after completing their education. The king called them one by one to enquire about their intellectual acquisitions.

'What have you studied?' he asked Jay.

'I have studied politics and have acquired mastery in governance,' Jay said. The king was excited at Jay's feat and said, 'Great. You are now worthy of succeeding me when I get old and retire.'

He asked Vijay about his education.

Vijay said, 'I have acquired training in warfare. I can lead the army and protect our kingdom.'

The king said, 'Great, my son! It is a wonderful feat. We can depend on you for protecting our kingdom.'

The king then called Mahir and briefed him on the

achievements of his elder brothers. Then he asked him about his learning. Mahir said, 'I have acquired mastery in the art of stealing. I can steal anything from anywhere.'

Mahir's answer came as a shock to the king. He was not expecting his youngest son to learn something unlawful and unacceptable. His excitement died. He wanted to give Mahir a tight slap, but he kept his composure. He didn't let Mahir or the others around him sense how shaken he was from within.

The king said, 'God bless you, my son. Go and rest. I will test your learning later.'

The king, too, moved to his quarters, deeply anxious for Mahir. At the end of the day, after dinner, the king called Mahir and asked him to steal a bowl filled with water, on the top of a pitcher that was suspended over the bed on which the king was to sleep.

It was not easy. If Mahir lifted the bowl, it would shake, spilling water on the king, and thus waking him up.

But Mahir said, 'It is the easiest task. I am fine with it.'

Pretty sure that Mahir wouldn't be able to steal the bowl, the king slept. Jay, Vijay and the others in the palace slept as well.

Mahir got to work in the silence of the night. He stealthily collected some ash from the kitchen in a small bag. Then, he got a ladder, fixed it to the roof near the pitcher. He added the ashes bit by bit in the bowl. The ash eventually absorbed the water. Then, Mahir picked up the bowl with the king sleeping soundly below.

Next morning, Mahir came to the court and gave the bowl to his father, touching his feet obediently. The king was stunned at Mahir's sleight of hand. He had not anticipated that Mahir would steal the bowl from under his nose. He was now depressed at the possibility of facing embarrassment because of his son's skill.

'I am a revered king. My people honour me for my sense of justice. How can I have a son who steals?' the king rued.

But, despite his musings, he put up a composed face and said, 'Full marks, my son. You have passed your first test with distinction. Go and celebrate your success. I will call you when needed.'

After sending Mahir to celebrate, the king plotted to get rid of him. He had several breeds of horses in his stable but he didn't have a shyamkaran horse. The shaymkaran was a unique breed that had a white body but black ears. All kings fancied a shaymkaran but rarely ever got one.

Incidentally, the neighbouring King Adhiraj possessed a shyamkaran.

The king called Mahir and said, 'God has blessed us with great opulence. The only thing we don't have is a shyamkaran horse. Adhiraj, the king in our neighbourhood has one. I will be glad if you bring that shyamkaran for me.'

Mahipal thought that Mahir would never succeed in stealing the shyamkaran from Adhiraj, who guarded it more than his life. He hoped that in his efforts to steal the shaymkaran, Mahir would get killed and, thus, he would get rid of a spoilt son.

But Mahir was excited to hear his father's proposal. 'Bless me! I will return with the shyamkaran in a few days,' Mahir said, touching his father's feet. He then set out on a mission to steal the rare horse.

After crossing his kingdom's boundary, Mahir, disguised as a beggar, reached Adhiraj's court. He touched Adhiraj's feet and begged for a job. Adhiraj, too, was a benevolent king. He asked the 'beggar', 'What would you like to do?'

Mahir said, 'I can do many things. But I love training horses the most.'

Adhiraj instantly asked Mahir to join his stable and take care of the horses. Mahir built a rapport with the horses in a short time. He recognized each horse by its name. The animals too responded to him. Soon, he established himself as a magnificent trainer. The horses trained by him won many races, elevating the king's name and fame.

Adhiraj had a daughter who loved riding horses. She developed a fascination for the horses especially trained by the 'beggar'. She fancied Mahir's company too. The princess had a beautiful face and curvaceous figure. She had captivating eyes and silky hair flowing down to her waistline. She was also talkative and witty.

But Mahir didn't fall for the princess's charm. Rather, he remained passionately involved in training the horses. He had, so far, no access to the shyamkaran, which lived separately under the care of an old and trusted trainer of Adhiraj.

Gradually, Mahir too, won the king's confidence and slowly plotted to get access to the shyamkaran. A clever thief, he knew that he was better positioned than the old trainer because he was liked by the princess too.

Mahir went to Adhiraj and said, 'I want to leave my job.' The king was stunned. 'What are you saying? We all love you so much. We appreciate your work and pay you well. What has prompted you to take this decision?'

Mahir calmly said, 'I would have enjoyed serving the shyamkaran. But I can't pursue my passion, for I have no access to the horse of my liking.' Adhiraj instantly allowed Mahir to serve the shyamkaran.

Apart from being a clever thief, Mahir was a great trainer of horses as well. He put the shyamkaran on more appropriate and advanced workout sessions. The shyamkaran's build improved and it could now gallop at a faster pace. He responded to his new trainer's commands very well.

One day, Mahir rode the shyamkaran and fled. Adhiraj's soldiers immediately followed the horse carrying Mahir. But the shyamkaran galloped with lightning speed, faster than all others, crossing the boundary of Adhiraj's kingdom in no time. Adhiraj's soldiers returned disappointed. Adhiraj and his army had no clue about where Mahir had taken the shyamkaran.

Mahir reached his father's palace and tied the shyamkaran in his stable. The next morning, he appeared in his father's court, announcing, 'Your wish is fulfilled. The shyamkaran is in our stable now.'

Mahipal was taken aback. He also knew that Adhiraj would not sit silent and eventually figure out where his shyamkaran was. 'Adhiraj has a friendly relationship with me. But once he finds out that my son has stolen his shyamkaran, he might attack our kingdom, causing undue damage and destruction. What explanation will I give him?' Mahipal mused.

Without informing Mahir, the conscientious king wrote a letter to Adhiraj and sent it to him through a messenger. The letter read, 'Honourable King Adhiraj, my son has brought your shyamkaran to me. Don't worry. Your horse is safe with us. You can take it back whenever you wish to.'

Adhiraj was overwhelmed with the honesty displayed by his neighbour. He wrote back, 'Honourable King Mahipal, your son is an excellent trainer of horses. He is not a mean thief. Rather, he is a scholar in the art of stealing, which we appreciate. I am offering my daughter's hand in marriage to Mahir. Please accept the shyamkaran as my wedding gift to your son. Let my daughter and your son enjoy riding the shyamkaran.'

Mahipal's joy knew no bounds when he got Adhiraj's letter.

He organized a grand wedding procession, reaching Adhiraj's palace with Mahir on the shyamkaran's back. The princess was very keen on marrying Mahir. The wedding ceremony took place in a joyful atmosphere. The prince and princess lived happily ever after.

Judge a man by his motives, not his actions.

THE GREATEST FOLK TALES OF BIHAR

The Mahout and the Dogs

Elephants, horses and camels were very important in wedding celebrations in villages. They acted as status symbols. The affluent landowners would arrange hordes of these animals and walk with their heads held high in society.

While on the one hand, the upper-caste landowners couldn't do without the elephants, horses and camels, the lower castes couldn't afford such luxury. They simply dreamt of seeing these exotic animals at wedding celebrations. But once they got rich, they, too, arranged for them to make their parties more colourful.

As it happened, a rich villager arranged for several elephants, horses and camels at his son's wedding. One of the elephants, with a mahout on its back, got hungry and went to feast on the leaves of a Pipal tree in the field at the village.

There lived several mischievous dogs in the village. They would always bark collectively when they saw elephants, making the children laugh hysterically. Usual to their habit, several dogs gathered around the elephant, busy eating the Pipal leaves, and began barking around it. The mahout continued sitting lazily on its back without doing a thing about it as the dogs were not disturbing him—only the elephant.

The elephant, which was calmly feasting on the leaves, got disturbed. She stretched out her trunk in the direction of the dogs, lifting one of them, and began waving it in the air. After waving the dog for a while, the elephant threw it up in the air.

But the dog fell on the mahout who was sitting on the elephant's back and bit him all over. Twirled and thrown by the elephant, the dog was in a frenzy. It violently dug its teeth into multiple parts of the mahout's body. The villagers took the wounded mahout to a vaidya. The mahout went through several months of treatment to get well.

If you do not pay heed to the first sign of trouble, it can soon become unmanageable.

THE GREATEST FOLK TALES OF BIHAR

Bharbitan

There lived a dwarf man named Bharbitan in a certain village. The name 'Bharbitan' denoted a man of abnormally short stature. The villagers had named him thus because he was below four feet in height.

Bharbitan lived with his two brothers, who had wives and children. He was unmarried because no woman agreed to marry a dwarf.

He led a miserable life. His brothers and sisters-in-law treated him like a slave. He would set out to herd buffaloes early in the morning and live solely on fruits and roots in the forest. He would eat whatever his sisters-in-law gave him when he returned at the end of the day. At times, he would sleep on an empty stomach.

Anguished, he shared his troubles with the villagers once. The villagers were kind to Bharbitan. They wanted him to live with due dignity. They organized a panchayat, which decided to get him separated from the family that disregarded him.

He got a buffalo and a small portion of the ancestral house in his share. From that day, he began herding his buffalo, milking it and cooking his own food. He had a relatively better

127

life after separation from his family.

One day, Bharbitan was herding his buffalo in the forest. Suddenly, the animal discharged a huge heap of dung, thus drowning Bharbitan. The buffalo then moved on, leaving Bharbitan suffocating in the heap that had covered him.

Bharbitan didn't return home that evening. There was no trace of Bharbitan the next morning either. His family members thought he had died. They cried and wept to show that they were mournful. But they were happy in their heart. They stealthily set the portion in which Bharbitan lived on fire after taking out all his belongings. They also dangled the skin of a dead buffalo at his door to convince him that his buffalo had died in case he returned.

Meanwhile, Bharbitan lay buried in the heap. Incidentally, a girl went to the forest to gather leaves and cattle dung for fuel. She removed the heap to find a dwarf suffocating in it. She rescued Bharbitan who narrated what had happened with him. She belonged to a poor family. But she was kind and took him home to care for him.

Served and cared for diligently by the girl, Bharbitan regained his health and returned to his village. Unlike his family, the villagers were excited to see him. They were kind to Bharbitan. They asked his family members to keep Bharbitan with them and take care of him till he regained his health and was able to live on his own again. His brothers brought Bharbitan home but their wives began torturing him again. Bharbitan was back to herding the buffaloes and living an ignominious life.

One day, the women asked him to catch birds from the forest for cooking. Bharbitan wandered for hours in the forest but failed to catch even one. He knew that his sisters-in-law would get livid if he returned empty-handed. Helpless, he began weeping.

As it happened, Lord Shiva and his consort, Goddess Parvati, were travelling through the forest. Seeing the dwarf weep, the kind-hearted goddess asked Shiva to enquire what had happened with the poor mortal. Shiva initially ignored her but gradually gave in to the Goddess's insistence.

As Shiva approached him, Bharbitan narrated his plight to the God. Shiva then gave him a mantra. 'If you chant *"Shivji ka sat"* (O Shiva, get him stuck) at your targets, they will get stuck where they are. And if you chant *"Shivji ka chhut"* (O Shiva, get them untangled), they will get untangled.' Shiva asked him to use the mantra wisely to his advantage.

Bharbitan chanted, *'Shivji ka sat'* at the birds fluttering around. Several birds got stuck where they were. Bharbitan gathered them and took them to his sisters-in-law. But the women rejected the birds. 'How have you managed to catch so many birds with their feathers and skin intact? It appears you have gathered dead birds,' one of them said and threw the birds in the debris.

His brothers joined their wives and beat Bharbitan black and blue. Bharbitan fled and lived at a villager's home that night. He sulked and decided to use Shiva's mantra to take revenge on his family members. Next morning, he reached home, only to find that his brothers were sleeping with their wives. Seething in anger, Bharbitan whispered, *'Shivji ka sat.'* His brothers and their wives got entangled in bed. Bharbitan, posing ignorant of their fate, hung around in the village.

As the day advanced, the neighbours realized that the dwarf's family members were still sleeping. They used all tricks to disentangle the family members. But nothing worked. The villagers asked Bharbitan to call a vaidya. But as the vaidya stepped in, Bharbitan whispered, *'Shivji ka sat.'* The vaidya got stuck to the door. Then a hakim was called. Bharbitan whispered '*Shivji ka sat*' and the hakim too got stuck.

Some wise villagers guessed that Bharbitan might have played a trick to teach his cruel family members a lesson. They bowed before him, requesting him to disentangle his family members. His brothers and sisters-in-law, too, folded their hands from their beds requesting Bharbitan to pardon them. Eventually, Bharbitan's heart softened and he chanted, '*Shivji ka chhut*.' They were freed.

His family members asked Bharbitan to live with them and promised him honour and dignity. But Bharbitan refused their gesture as he preferred to live separately.

One day, he took the buffalo's skin dangling at his door to sell in the market. But by the time he reached the forest on his way, it became dark. Bharbitan climbed a tree, thinking he would resume his journey the next morning. He saw a group of thieves gathered below, sharing the booty they had stolen from someone's house. He dropped the buffalo's skin on the thieves. They thought that some ghost had struck them in the desolate woods and were petrified. They fled, abandoning their treasures—jewels, money, utensils and grains.

Bharbitan bundled up all the assets and returned home. When his brothers asked him how he had gotten so much wealth, Bharbitan said that he had bought them with the money he had got by selling the skin.

His greedy brothers decided to do what Bharbitan had done to become rich. They killed the two buffaloes they had and took their skin to sell.

But they got a meagre amount for the skin. They became poorer as they had killed their buffaloes—major sources of their income. On the other hand, Bharbitan got his house renovated, bought two oxen and a bullock cart. He loaded the rubbish

130

and charcoal—remains of his burnt house—in his bullock cart and headed for the market to sell them off.

It was night again when he reached the forest on the way. Bharbitan tied his oxen and parked his cart in a corner. While resting, he spotted two traders setting up a camp near him. The traders, too, had a bullock cart loaded with goods. Bharbitan inquired about their trade. They said that they traded in gold and silver which were loaded in their cart. Bharbitan then said, 'I trade in diamond and pearls, which are loaded in my cart.'

After Bharbitan was in a deep sleep, the traders found Bharbitan's bullock cart and drove it away. When Bharbitan woke up, he saw that the traders had left their own cart. He took their cart to his house. The cart was full of gold and silver. Bharbitan turned rich overnight. He got a magnificent house built and employed several servants to look after him and his property.

He remembered the girl who had rescued him from the heap of dung. He proposed to marry her and she happily agreed. Bharbitan forgave the way his brothers and their wives had treated him and allowed them to live with him and his wife in the magnificent house.

Everyone can reach great heights with hard work and a positive attitude.

PRANKS, INTRIGUES, STRUGGLE AND ENTERTAINMENT

Bhikhari Thakur's Popular Folklores

Gabarghichor

Galeej, a youth hailing from a low caste, got married to a woman of the same caste and equal status. She was from to the neighbouring village. He brought his bride in a palanquin—a local band party in tow—and began living with her in a small hut in his village.

The pangs of poverty did not allow marital bliss to last long. He soon left for the city in search of livelihood, leaving his wife behind. She began working in the agriculture fields and managed to make ends meet by planting paddy seedlings, sowing wheat seeds and removing weed from landowners' plots. She was beautiful, but her poverty had weighed her down, robbing her off her youthful exuberance.

Weeks turned into months and months into years. The woman waited for her husband to return. She nurtured the dream that her man would come one day, bringing her garments and jewellery. She grieved for him every day. But Galeej did not return even after fifteen years.

Eventually, in Galeej's long absence, his wife and another youth, Gadbadi, got into a physical relationship and a son was born. The villagers named the boy Gabarghichor—a name questioning the legitimacy of his birth. But she raised him with all her motherly care and love.

As the years passed, Gabarghichor turned thirteen, and began accompanying his mother to the farms and helping her with her chores. With a son in the house, the woman was no longer lonely. However, some villagers made snide remarks, teasing Gabarghichor and describing his mother as a woman of easy virtue. But it made no difference to the mother and son, who shared a bond of love and trust.

As it so happened, a villager went to the city where Galeej was working and updated him on the affairs at home. Galeej was living a wretched existence in the city. He pulled a *thela* for a living and squandered whatever he earned on country liquor and prostitutes. He had almost forgotten his wife and home.

As the villager told him about his wife and son, he was filled with nostalgia. He got excited to learn that he had been 'blessed' with a son who was grown up now. The villager advised him to return to the village and take care of his family.

'If I bring my son to the city, he can work with me and increase our earnings. We could live a better life,' Galeej thought and instantly left for his village. His wife's joy knew no bounds when she saw her husband after many long years. She introduced Gabarghichor to his father and asked him to touch his feet. Galeej hugged him warmly.

After a couple of days, Galeej asked his wife to let Gabarghichor go with him to the city. The wife objected, 'I suffered immense loneliness in your absence. I survived because of Gabarghichor. You should live with us and give up the idea of going back to the city.'

Gabarghichor agreed with his mother. 'What is the harm if all of us live together in the village? But if you still insist to take me, take my mother along too. I won't go alone with you.'

The ephemeral bonhomie between the couple fell like ninepins. The wife and husband broke into a vicious quarrel. While Galeej and his wife were fighting, Gadbadi, who lived in the neighbourhood, came to claim Gabarghichor.

'You lived in the city for fifteen years. Gabarghichor was born and grew up in your absence. How can you claim my son? I have fathered Gabaghichor, which you can confirm with your wife', Gadbadi said to Galeej.

Galeej turned to his wife. The woman said, 'Yes, I slept with Gadbadi once in a moment of loneliness. But that does not mean Gabarghichor is Gadbadi's son. Gabarghichor was born from my womb. I am his mother, and hence, I am the sole custodian of my son'.

Unable to sort out their differences, Gadbadi, Galeej and the woman agreed to call a *panch* to settle the issue. The panch—an upper caste Brahmin commonly referred to as Baba—came to settle the row.

The panch first called Gadbadi, asking him angrily, 'How can you claim to be Gabarghichor's father? Are you married to the woman? Has anyone seen you tie the knot with her? Has anyone attended your wedding party? How can you prove that Gabarghichor is your son?'

Gadbadi pleaded, 'Baba! Listen to me patiently. Suppose I get an empty wallet lying abandoned on the streets. I fill it with my money. Later, the actual owner of the wallet comes in and identifies his wallet. What should I do?'

After a pause, when the panch didn't answer, Gadbadi replied to his own question, 'I should take out my money and give the wallet back to the owner. Thus, you should allow my asset Gabarghichor to be with me and the woman can be with Galeej'.

The panch pondered over Gadbadi's plea. He asked Galeej to put forth his point. Galeej argued, 'Gadbadi is talking

137

nonsense. Suppose I sow a seed of pumpkin in my courtyard and its stems and shoots spread out to the neighbour's hut. If my plant bears a fruit on the neighbour's hut, it does not belong to the neighbour. The fruit belongs to the owner of the plant.'

The panch now called the woman, asking her to explain her stand. She said, 'Galeej and Gadbadi are talking rubbish. Gabarghichor was born from my womb. Imagine, I have a bucketful of milk. If someone adds a pinch of *joran* to help process the milk into curd, he can't claim the entire curd. Gadbadi can't claim Gabarghichor just because he lent me a few drops of his *virya*. Gabarghichor is mine.'

'It is a tricky situation. What is the way out?' the panch mused.

Gadbadi, Galeej and the woman again broke into a squabble. The other elders of the village joined them, asking them to wait patiently for the panch's decision. 'Once you have called a panch, you must cooperate with him in reaching a conclusion,' a village elder said, asking the panch to settle the row.

The panch resumed the negotiation process. He asked Gabarghichor, 'Who do you want to live with? What is your wish?'

Gabarghichor said, 'If you allow me to have my wish, I will prefer to live with my mother. But I will agree to whatever you decide.'

Now, the panch called the woman to ask her why she had slept with another man. The woman argued, 'Gadbadi would come to my door every morning and evening with a sad face. He repeatedly begged me... Like me, he, too, lived alone. He suggested we have pleasure to beat our boredom. Once, I yielded to his persuasion. *Itna hi toh baat hai* (That is all there is to it).'

Gadbadi and Galeej, guessing that the panch was inclined towards the woman, thought of bribing the panch.

Gadbadi cornered the panch and offered him ₹200 for letting Gabarghichor be with him. Galeej, then, cornered the panch and offered him ₹500 to get the decision in his favour.

Noticing that the two men were trying to bribe the panch, the woman came forward to plead, 'Baba! I have no money to give. But if you let my son be with me, I will be obliged to you and serve you my entire life.'

But the panch took the bribe from both Gadbadi and Galeej, pronouncing his judgement, 'Gabarghichor should be hacked into three equal pieces to be shared among Gadbadi, Galeej and the woman. Gabarghichor belongs to all three and no one can claim sole custody on him.'

Gadbadi and Galeej accepted the decision. Gabarghichor was made to sleep on the ground and a butcher was called to hack him into three equal pieces. The villagers gathered to see the act of 'justice'.

As the butcher whipped out his knife, the woman intervened, pleading to the panch, 'Baba! Listen to me before my son is slaughtered.'

The panch said, 'What do you want to say now? The decision has been made.'

She said, 'I am a mother. I can't see the son I've raised with so much love and hardship getting slaughtered before my eyes. It is better you give him either to Gadbadi or Galeej. I withdraw my claim on him.'

The panch realized that the mother was the only one of the three who really loved and cared for him. He announced, 'Gabarghichor will remain with his mother. Both Galeej and Gadbadi are sinners. They should be ostracized by society and driven out of the village.'

Decisions taken with wit and wisdom always lead to justice.

The Daughter's Suffering

Upato was the young daughter of Lobha and Chatak—a couple from a lower caste. Upato was the lifeline of the family. She worked in the fields, drew water from the well and cooked food.

The family lived in a cluster of huts with other people of the low caste. The villagers toiled hard for their bare survival. A full meal of rice, roti, dal and vegetables was a dream. They often had to do with a meal of rice, onion, chilli and salt to fill their stomachs. They could afford minimal clothes—enough to cover the essential parts of their body.

Upato's world was confined to working in the fields, herding goats, collecting cattle droppings and leaves for fuel and cooking food. She was calm and quiet, and avoided quarrels. If at all she raised her voice, it was to control her goats when they strayed. Her parents called her Lakshmi—the Goddess of wealth—to praise her conduct.

When she blossomed into a fine woman, she began drawing the attention of her community members. The villagers began putting pressure on Chatak and Lobha to marry her off. In the village, if a daughter reached marriageable age, she often became everyone's concern. A woman of marriageable age living in her parent's home was frowned upon by the villagers.

Panditji and the *hajam* of the village invariably worked as intermediaries in the marriages that would take place in the village. 'Upato is old enough to get married,' Panditji would tell Chatak. The barber, too, would poke Chatak to fulfil his obligation to his daughter. The women often badgered Lobha, asking her if they were looking for a groom. Due to these constant reminders, Lobha and Chatak became anxious about their daughter's marriage.

Once, when they had finished their dinner and gone to sleep, Lobha confessed to her husband, 'The neighbours are pointing fingers at us now. You should look for a groom for Upato. How long will we keep our daughter with us?' Chatak murmured, 'I am anxious about it as well. What inhibits me is our poverty. After all, marriages require money. We are supposed to give at least a sari to the bride and a dhoti-kurta to the groom for dowry. Besides, we will have to feed the *baratis* and our neighbours. These requirements weigh heavy on my head.'

While Chatak and Lobha were struggling for the wherewithal needed to marry off their daughter, Panditji came up with a proposal for Upato. 'I have a groom in mind for Upato. He is very wealthy,' Panditji said. Chatak found Panditji's words reassuring—like an oasis in a desert.

His eyes twinkling, Chatak said, 'Tell me about him.'

Panditji said, 'The groom's name is Jhantul and he lives alone in a big house at Baklol village, a few miles away. He has a big chunk of farmland and several cows and buffaloes. Your daughter will live like a queen with him.'

Chatak enquired, 'If he is so wealthy, why will he accept our daughter in marriage? We are so poor. I don't think he will agree.'

Panditji said, 'He is an old man and ailing too. He is looking for a woman to look after him in his advancing age.' Chatak sank into a contemplative mood. 'Why should we give our daughter to an old man? It will be injustice to Upato,' Chatak thought.

After a long pause, Panditji said, 'Jhantul is ready to pay ₹1,600 if you agree to marry your daughter to him.' On hearing the amount, the greed in Chatak overcame the hesitation clouding his mind. He immediately agreed. At this stage, Panditji said, 'I have worked very hard to set up this offer. You will have to pay me ₹200 after the wedding.'

Chatak never earned beyond ₹10 despite toiling hard on the landlord's fields all day. And that, too, was never certain. An amount of ₹1600 was too good an offer to refuse. He didn't remember when he had seen a hundred-rupee note.

He knew that the villagers would disgrace him for selling off his daughter for ₹1600. People who sold their daughters were known as *beti bechwas* in the village. They were looked down upon. But it was not very uncommon in the impoverished society of the village. Keeping everything in mind, Chatak agreed to Panditji's proposal.

As night fell, he discussed the proposal with his wife. Lobha resisted it. But Chatak argued, 'We are so poor. After all, Lobha will go to a wealthy home. We will get ₹1,600 that will enable us to release our land from the moneylender's possession. We will have relief from poverty.'

Lobha fell prey to Chatak's persuasion. But she pointed out the ignominy they would suffer. 'People will call us "beti bechwas". We will lose respect in the community.'

Chatak suggested a way out. 'You shouldn't discuss it in the community,' he said. Chatak was sure that Panditji would not discuss it for he was involved in the bargain.

Upato was young and beautiful. But the mist of poverty had reduced her hopes. She didn't dream big. She didn't even know what a queen-like life would be like. She had thought that her parents would find a groom who was of her age and was able enough to work on the farms. She had dreamt of a life partner who would connect with her. But she had always thought all this to herself. She had never discussed any of this with her parents. Chatak and Lobha had not discussed anything with her either.

Panditji fixed an auspicious date for the wedding. The bridegroom came with huge pomp and show at Upato's doorstep. The villagers gathered around to see the groom. Jhantul was an old man and was unable to even walk. Wobbling, he reached the hut that was decorated with flowers, and mango and banana leaves.

Upato was shocked beyond words when she saw Jhantul from a corner. But she sulked and sobbed in silence. Panditji, assisted by the barber, solemnized the marriage, observing all the rituals. The women sang songs throughout the wedding, which lasted the entire night. Upato wept uncontrollably when she was sent off with her husband the next morning. Her heart had sunk into a deep abyss. Meanwhile, looking at the groom, the villagers talked in hushed voices.

After the *vidai* ceremony, Panditji reminded Upato's parents about the ₹200 that Chatak owed him as part the 'deal'. Chatak said, 'Baba! The guests are still around. Come some other time.' Lobha touched his feet, saying, 'We are poor. Please don't press for ₹200; it is a big amount for us. Have mercy on us.'

The wily Panditji sensed that the couple might deny him the amount and started narrating loudly how he had managed to extract ₹1,600 from Jhantul for their daughter. The villagers

143

heard the entire story and came to know that Chatak and Lobha had sold off their daughter to an old man. They left their house, abusing them and shouting 'beti bechwa'.

On the other hand, life turned from bad to worse for Upato. Pinned down by old-age infirmities, Jhantul wanted Upato to massage his aching limbs and escort him to the bathroom. She had to make him stand up and sit down every now and then. Jhantul was of her grandfather's age. There was, of course, enough grain, milk and curd at Jhantul's home to feast on. But Jhantul had nothing that Upato had hoped for in her future husband.

Upato felt suffocated and got depressed. Once, when he was asleep, Upata left him and returned to her parents. 'He doesn't have a single tooth in his mouth. He is hard of hearing and seeing. He can't eat rice and roti. He drinks liquids for all his meals. He can't stand up or sit down on his own. He can collapse any day. I won't live with him.' Upato begged her parents to take her back.

But Jhantul followed her. He came in his bullock cart complaining how Upato had acted in a way that was unbecoming of a wife. 'I am an old man but she is utterly cruel. She has come to you without caring about who will feed me. After all, I have given her everything,' Jhantul screamed in exasperation.

Chatak pleaded with his daughter, 'After your wedding, your husband is your God. You have got what destiny had in store for you. You should dedicate your life to your husband.' Lobha counselled, 'Don't be sinful and silly. Jhantul has given you everything—a good house to live in, plenty of food to eat and clothes to wear—except youthfulness, which he doesn't have any more.'

The parents forced her to go back with her husband. Upato

left her home crying that she would never return. 'I will now believe that my mother and father are dead. What I thought was my village is nothing more than a mound of lifeless people for me,' she screamed while leaving.

The villagers, this time, sympathized with Lobha and Chatak. 'Of course, Lobha and Chatak committed a grave sin by marrying off their daughter to an old man. But Upato should now live with her husband. Destiny can't be changed,' said a village elder. The priest and barber concurred.

Upato sulked in silence for days, adjusting to what destiny had given her at Jhantul's home. Gripped by multiple infirmities, her ageing husband was too seized with old age to take care of his wife. But Upato had no complaints now because she had no one to fall back on. She had accepted that there was no escape for her from this life.

After a few months, Jhantul died. His death had, in fact, brought deliverance to her. She was free from serving a man she never had any emotional attachment to.

But her husband's death turned her into a widow—an inauspicious being. She didn't have children. It doubled the stigma—a widow without a child was a bigger curse. The Baklol villagers would look down upon her. 'Jhantul died within a year of his marriage with her. She has turned out to be a husband-eater,' the villagers would say.

She found it burdensome to manage the house, cattle and fields of her husband. She had no interest in property. She detested the grain sacks, cattle and crops. She was ready to exchange that with peace and two meals every day.

Years passed as Upato continued living with the belongings she hated. She turned old. She found managing the cattle and farmlands taxing and her limbs began to ache.

Once, she called her husband's nephew, Udbas, and his

145

wife, and gave them all the belongings in exchange for two meals every day. Udbas and his wife were overjoyed. They saw in Upato—their *kaki*—Goddess Lakshmi smiling on them. They looked after her well, giving her immense respect apart from food and clothes.

Udbas and his wife gave her what she had craved for years after Jhantul's death. Satisfied with their conduct, Upato decided to give more to them. One day, she handed over the keys of the kitchen and store to the couple and formally registered the land and house in their name. But as soon as Udbas and his wife became owners of Upato's property, their behaviour towards her changed. They became less caring towards Upato.

Once, a mendicant came to their door, seeking alms. Upato gave a coin of four paisa to the beggar. Then all hell broke loose. 'Why did she give alms to the beggar without asking us? Now that we are the owners of the property, she should have asked us before spending anything,' Udbas's wife complained to her husband.

She yelled, 'Upato is a widow without any children. She is inauspicious.' Udbas initially tried to pacify his wife. 'She is an old woman. There is nothing wrong in gifting something to a mendicant. After all, everything we own is given by her. You should not get angry with her,' Udbas counselled his wife.

But the woman was not ready to budge. 'Either she lives here or I live with you. You have to make a choice,' his wife declared and stopped eating.

Udbas was faced with a dilemma. It was hard for him to leave his wife for his kaki and it was down right sinful to kick kaki out to keep his wife's whims. Udbas went to his friend Updesh for consultation.

Initially, Updesh suggested that it was unethical to disown the old woman who had given all her belongings to them. But when Udbas told him that his wife had asked him to make a choice between kaki and her, Updesh, too, thought it wise for Udbas to acquiesce to his wife's wish.

Updesh came up with an idea. 'Your wife and you should take kaki to a pilgrimage and abandon her in the crowd. That way, your wife's wish will be fulfilled and you will live merrily with all her belongings as well.'

Udbas agreed and asked Updesh to accompany them on the pilgrimage. He shared the idea with his wife and announced the news of the pilgrimage to kaki. Upato was very happy to go on a pilgrimage with her nephew-in-law and his wife. Udbas, Updesh and Udbas's wife left for the pilgrimage with Upato.

The sun had set and the night had begun when they reached a forest on the way to the pilgrimage. They halted and camped near a river in the forest so that they could resume the journey as soon as the dawn broke. When he was going to sleep, Udbas decided to kill Upato in the silence of the forest. He discussed the idea with Updesh, who approved it.

Now, Udbas, with a sharp sickle in his hands, and Updesh following him, approached Upato. Upato, who was dreaming about the pilgrimage site, suddenly woke up and got scared to see a sickle in Udbas's hand. She sensed what Udbas was up to.

'Spare my life. I beg of you. I will wash your clothes. I will cook food for you both. I will do everything you tell me to do. I will not spend a penny without your permission,' Upato begged.

In a fit of shock, she screamed, 'O Lord Krishna! Where are you? O God! Have mercy on me.' Hearing her loud wails, a saint who was nearby came over to them, a trident in his hands. Udbas, his wife and Updesh fled when they saw the saint. He asked Upato the reasons for her trauma.

Upato narrated her plight to the saint, who took her to his

cottage. He got another cottage built for Upato and advised her to forget the world and give her life to the devotion of Lord Krishna to get 'lasting liberation' from the world's maya.

Greed for material things can make people do horrible things.

The Lore of Love

Saranga and Sadabrij

Once upon a time there lived a Brahmin priest Devdatta and his wife Kamalvati in a place called Ambavati. The couple devoted most of their time to prayer. Kamalavati was a *pativrata* and ate food only after worshipping her husband. Devdatta, too, cared for her immensely.

They had adequate land and cattle to live happily and even donate. But they didn't have children. The couple prayed to Lord Shiva for a son. As the years passed, they got anxious about who would inherit their property and legacy after them.

Once, a saint came to their door, seeking alms. Devdatta proposed, 'We are in the last leg of our lives. We don't have anyone to inherit our property. We will be pleased if you accept our belongings in the name of Lord Shiva and liberate us from worldly bondage.'

The saint accepted the offer and said, 'You have prayed to Lord Shiva your entire life. I bless you to live as husband and wife in your next 12 lives too.' Having blessed the couple, the saint disappeared. They donated all their assets to the saint and died in piece after the hermit left.

Devdatta and Kamalvati were born into two different castes

in their next birth and got into a loving relationship when they grew up. But the social barrier prevented them from marrying. They got depressed and died by immolating themselves.

Since they had committed 'sin' by committing suicide, they were denied births as human beings and were born as monkeys in a desolate forest. The male and the female monkey married but died after falling into a pond from a tree.

In the next birth, the male monkey was born as Suryabhan in a rich landlord's family in Kanchanpur village. The parents celebrated the son's birth by donating generously to the Brahmins and beggars. The female monkey, on the other hand, was born as a *pari* at Lord Indra's palace in the heavens and was named Rambha. Fairies or apsaras are companions of gods. They are known for their enchanting beauty, magical powers, and dancing and singing skills. Rambha was stunningly beautiful and enjoyed Lord Indra's special attention.

When Rambha turned twelve, she received the supernatural ability to change her form whenever she wished. She would often travel to earth without Indra's knowledge. One day, she went to the Kanchanpur garden, full of blossoming flowers. The garden belonged to Suryabhan, who was strolling there when Rambha descended. But Suryabhan was unaware of her presence. He was tired and decided to sit on a bench. Rambha saw Suryabhan and was awestruck by his handsomeness. She almost swooned when she saw him but controlled herself. She got close to him and jingled her ornaments to wake Suryabhan.

When Suryabhan woke up, he was mesmerized to see Rambha. Stunned, Suryabhan said, 'The aroma of sandalwood is wafting from you. Your lips resemble a blossoming lotus. I can't take my eyes off you. Your gaze has pierced my heart.'

Hearing Suryabhan's honeyed words, Rambha said, 'You are so sweet. Your forehead glows more than that of Indra. I am unable to control myself after seeing you.'

Rambha surrendered herself to Suryabhan. Suryabhan and Rambha were wrapped in each other's arms. But Suryabhan restrained himself, separating himself from Rambha. He pleaded, 'We are not supposed to make love before marrying.'

Rambha garlanded Suryabhan, accepting him as her husband with the sun, sky and earth as their witnesses. 'The Vedas and shastras have sanctioned our marriage with the sun, sky and earth as witnesses,' Rambha said.

Thereafter, Rambha and Suryabhan cuddled with each other and made love. Their warm breaths caressed their necks. Rambha stroked Suryabhan's hair and Suryabhan sucked her lips.

After sometime, Rambha stated the urgency to return to Indra's palace. 'I have come without Indra's permission, so I have to go back to his palace. Don't lose heart as I will come back again,' she said.

'But you are my wife now. Why should you go to Indra? Where does Indra live? Who is he? Why can't I go with you?' Suryabhan argued.

Rambha pleaded, 'Indra is the king of all Gods. Only Gods and Goddesses live in his palace. I am a fairy bound by my duty to dance and sing when Indra holds his durbar. The place is forbidden for the denizens of the earth.'

Suryabhan held Rambha, begging, 'I will die if you leave me.'

Rambha was in a dilemma. Using her magical power, she converted Suryabhan into a bumblebee and concealed him between her breasts, covered with her choli. Then, she flew off to heaven.

It was time for Indra's durbar. Other fairies had performed. It was Rambha's turn. She began dancing and singing. In the middle of her performance, she felt the bumblebee suffocating inside. Rambha paused and loosened her garments to relieve the bumblebee. But her rhythm broke, angering Indra. A courtier sensed that Rambha was concealing something and complained about it to Indra. The king of Gods found the bumblebee in her clothes.

He blazed in anger, 'How did you dare to bring a mortal creature into heaven?'

Rambha said, 'I had gone to a garden to pluck flowers for puja. I don't know how the bumblebee crept in my clothes.'

But Indra sensed her mischief. He sprinkled holy water on the bumblebee, bringing it to its original form. Overwhelmed by Indra, Suryabhan narrated how Rambha had come to his garden and how they had gotten married. Infuriated, Indra cursed them to die instantly. But Rambha fell on his feet, seeking mercy.

Indra then commanded, 'Both of you will be born as animals and birds in your next three births. After that, the spell of my curse will end and both of you will be born as woman and man to resume your life journey.'

Saying this, Indra dropped the duo from heaven to earth and they both died. After wandering through three births as jackals, parrots and swans, Rambha was born as a woman in the Gwala caste, and Suryabhan as a man in the Koiri caste.

As ordained in their previous births, they fell in love. They would often meet each other. But their family members noticed their 'unholy' affair and killed them. They were born as men and women thrice in different castes and suffered violent deaths in a similar manner.

On his twelfth birth, Suryabhan was born to Jayanti and Jagdish—Rajput queen and king of the kingdom of Ambavati. Jagdish and Jayanti were pious people. Their subjects loved them for their generosity. Blessed with a son, they organized a grand feast and called astrologers and priests to name their son and predict his future. The chief priest named the newborn Sadabrij, professing, 'Sadabrij is an incarnation of love. He will become famous but will fall madly in love with a woman who was a fairy in her previous birth. He might become a hermit to win her love.'

They were upset to learn about the foreboding prophecy but shrugged off the anxiety in their happiness to receive a handsome son. Women sang *sohars* and musicians and artists performed exuberantly. Jagdish made generous donations to priests and beggars to celebrate the occasion.

Rambha was born to Padmavati and Padumshah, a rich merchant couple from the Bania community living in the same kingdom. Padumshah owned several palaces and gardens. He, too, invited astrologers to the party he had thrown to celebrate the daughter's birth. The astrologers named her Saranga and professed that she would grow into a stunning beauty as she had been a fairy in her previous life. Padmavati and Padumshah were thrilled to learn about their daughter.

Sadabrij and Saranga were admitted into the same school. Saranga and Sadabrij were teenagers and hadn't seen each other before they stepped into the school. But they got intimate as soon as they met. They would bunk classes and stayed engrossed in conversations in the classroom. 'I can't keep my eyes off you. You are so pretty. I want to see you all the time,' Sadabrij said. 'I feel the same. I get restless when I am at home. I get solace only when I see you again. I love to talk to you,' Saranga said.

Once, Sadabrij left class to drink water in the garden and hinted to Saranga to follow him. Saranga followed him. Together, in privacy, they embraced each other. A student saw them clasped in each other's arms and informed the teacher who came out, scolding Saranga and Sadabrij, 'You are kids. You shouldn't spend so much time together away from class.'

Hearing the teacher's angry words, Saranga said, 'The level of water in the well had gone down. It took time to draw water and drink.' The teacher, however, had sensed that Saranga and Sadabrij were involved in a passionate relationship, which he found inappropriate at their unripe age.

The teacher thought of a ploy to keep them separated. He called a tailor and ordered him to suspend a thick curtain between Saranga and Sadabrij so that they couldn't see each other. But Saranga clandestinely bribed the tailor, suggesting him to punch a peephole in the curtain so that she and Sadabrij could see each other. The tailor did what he was told but others didn't notice it.

Saranga and Sadabrij would exchange glances through the curtain. The teacher also kept separate containers for boys and girls to drink water from. When Sadabrij's and Saranga's turn came, they reached there, hand in hand.

Saranga noticed a parrot pecking an unripe lemon and asked Sadabrij to replicate it on her. Sadabrij drew her closer and kissed her. Kissing her passionately, Sadabrij said, 'I am drawing the drops of nectar from your lips.' Saranga closed her eyes and whispered, 'I am lost in the pleasure of your lips on mine.' With this, they began caressing each other, locked in embrace.

The teacher visited the garden at that moment and was shocked to see them. He avoided using harsh words because they belonged to prestigious families. But he said in an innuendo, 'The parrot has been destroying the unripe lemon. The impetuous parrot should have waited for the fruit to ripen.' He wanted to tell Sadabrij and Saranga that they were destroying their lives before attaining the appropriate age.

Saranga blushed but said, 'O teacher! Sadabrij is a child, incapable of chewing lemon. I, too, am innocent. While watering the plants we got tired and slept under the shade of the tree.' Sadabrij was embarrassed to hear the dialogue between Saranga and the teacher.

The sun had gone down. The teacher asked them to go home and they obeyed. But after that, they kept meeting. Cosying up in the warmth of togetherness, they grew in age and shape. Once, they were strolling in the garden of the school premises. Sadabrij had his arms around Saranga's waist. Saranga had her arms on his shoulders. They were blissfully ignorant that the sun had set and darkness had settled in. They felt hungry. Sadabrij brought bananas which they fed to each other.

The birds stopped chirping as the night enveloped the surroundings. Sadabrij spread sheets of banana leaves to sleep on. They were unmarried and not supposed to make love. Sadabrij put a sword between Saranga and him and they slept. As the dawn broke and the day advanced, the school opened. The teacher was shocked to see them sleeping together.

'Why are you so shameless? You should respect social norms. Your conduct will hurt your families' honour,' the teacher screamed.

Saranga pleaded, 'We got tired of drawing water from the well to irrigate the plants. We slept with a sword between us. Don't doubt us.' Then, they left for their respective homes.

But the teacher was now convinced about their 'unholy' escapades. He met Padumshah and advised him to find a suitable groom for his daughter within his caste, revealing the affair between Saranga and Sadabrij.

Padumshah got anxious and asked his wife to counsel Saranga against getting intimate with a Rajput prince.

Padmavati counselled Saranga, 'Sadabrij is a Rajput prince. We belong to the Bania caste. A Bania girl and a Rajput prince cannot marry. Forget Sadabrij and prepare yourself to marry a suitable boy of our caste.'

Saranga said bluntly, 'O Mother! We can't live separately. What is there in caste? Our blood has the same colour. Love doesn't know caste. Thirst hardly differentiates between two streams. Hunger doesn't care whether the food is fresh or from the previous night. Sleep does not care if the bed is soft or hard.'

Padmavati got the message and told her husband that Saranga was beyond counselling. She asked him to find a suitable groom for her and forcibly marry her off as soon as possible. Padumshah went to Jagdish, apprising him of the affair between Saranga and Sadabrij. Jagdish and Padumshah shared a dignified relationship. Jagdish agreed to do what was necessary for their families' honour.

Padumshah suggested that the king send Sadabrij to Manikpur—a part of his estate—for two months to collect taxes. 'I will use the time to find a suitable groom for Saranga and marry her off,' he said. Jagdish agreed and ordered Sadabrij to go to Manikpur with his treasurer's son, Veersen, who was also Sadabrij's friend.

Sadabrij couldn't disobey his father. But he was shocked to learn that his father would not let him marry Saranga. Saranga, too, slipped into depression to learn that her parents had decided to marry her off to some other boy. She would sit near her window all day, waiting hopelessly to see Sadabrij pass by. She had no place for anyone else in her heart.

Sadabrij shared his feelings for Saranga with Veersen. Veersen promised to help him and suggested that Sadabrij take the route which had Saranga's home on his way to Manikpur.

Riding their horses, Sadabrij and Veersen went to Saranga's village. While Veersen waited at a distance, Sadabrij went near her home. As she saw Sadabrij from the window, she sang sadly, 'You are a dream for me now. My parents are forcibly marrying me off to another boy. It appears we will never meet now.'

Sadabrij sang back, 'Dear Saranga, don't lose heart. Have faith in the Almighty and look for ways to meet me. It is going to be a long toil for us from now on. But I won't marry anyone other than you my entire life.'

Sadabrij told Veersen that he couldn't live without Saranga. Veersen suggested, 'We should disguise ourselves as magicians wandering around Saranga's palace. I will befriend her relatives to gather information about her. Nobody will recognize us.'

After a few days, Padumshah selected Madhukar, the son of a rich merchant named Brajraj of Dhara Nagar, and fixed the wedding. The wedding party came with horses and elephants. The revellers burst crackers. Padumshah's mansion was bathed in the milky glow of light. Men and women danced on the beat of drums as the chariot carrying Madhukar reached Saranga's home. Though in bridal attire, Saranga sulked and sobbed.

While the relatives celebrated, Sadabrij and Veersen rode on their horses in the garb of magicians, charming the audience on their way. But Saranga recognized Sadabrij and sang, 'The flower has blossomed but the gardener has disowned it. The treacherous bumblebee is around to suck the flower that the gardener had nursed.'

Saranga's voice was drowned in the chorus of others singing and dancing. But Sadabrij heard it. He sang back, 'Have faith in your gardener. He is working hard for his flower. Don't sulk. The gardener won't let others suck his loving flower.' The revellers took Sadabrij's singing as one of his ways to charm them.

Sadabrij, regaling the audience, reached the groom's chariot as it entered through the door for the ceremonial puja and suggested the priest worship his sword first for the happiness of the bride and groom. The priest took Sadabrij's suggestion as some ritual and began worshipping the sword.

While his sword was being worshipped, Sadabrij vanished and got into the garb of a woman. The relatives took him to be a guest and let him go to Saranga. But Saranga knew that 'she' was her lover. He offered Saranga a necklace, whispering in her ears that he would come at the time of her wedding and sneak her out.

Later that evening, Sadabrij got into the garb of a comedian and went inside Saranga's home where she was sitting with her groom at the mandap and the priest was preparing for the ritual of *sindurdan*. Sadabrij asked the priest to first keep a pinch of vermilion on his sword, which the priest thought was a ritual and carried out. Others took Sadabrij as a comedian but Saranga recognized him. As the priest put vermillion on the sword, Saranga stealthily covered her fingers in vermillion and applied it on her forehead. Then the priest let Madhukar apply sindur on Saranga's forehead.

Realizing that the occasion was not the right time to talk to Saranga, Sadabrij surreptitiously suggested her to go to the Kali temple on the pretext of seeking Goddess Kali's blessings after her marriage. While the guests were feasting and the hosts were busy serving them, Saranga went to the temple, where Sadabrij was waiting for her. Sadabrij hugged her tightly. Saranga slipped into his arms, kissing him madly. 'I first wore the vermillion from your sword which means you are my real husband. Now take me away from my fake marriage with Madhukar,' Saranga begged Sadabrij.

Saranga suggested a way out, 'There is a Shiva temple one

kilometre away on the route which the wedding party will take tomorrow morning. Wait for me at the temple. I will meet you on the way to my in-laws' place.'

By the time they were done, Saranga realized she was late. It would be difficult to sneak in now. Sadabrij dressed her in a man's attire and asked her to change into her bridal dress after reaching home so that no one could notice the bride sneaking in. She followed his instructions.

Saranga's family members sent her off with tears in their eyes as dawn broke. She sat inside a palanquin, which the haulers lifted and moved. Madhukar, in a chariot, escorted her; others followed them.

Sadabrij covered himself in grey ashes, wore saffron, and carried a parrot in a cage in one hand and a trident in the other. In this attire, he reached the Shiva temple.

As the palanquin reached there, Saranga asked the carriers to stop for a while. 'I have worshipped Lord Shiva all my life. I want to pray one last time at this temple before I leave,' she said.

The palanquin stopped and Saranga hurried into the temple. But Sadabrij was asleep and her repeated calls fell on his deaf ears. Saranga asked the parrot, 'Is he drunk or has he smoked marijuana?'

The parrot said, 'O Dear Sister! He is neither drunk nor has he smoked marijuana. He got tired performing at your wedding party and has fallen asleep.'

Saranga drew blood by cutting her finger and wrote her address with it on a piece of cloth. She gave it to the parrot, asking him to give it to Sadabrij when he awoke. Saranga then came out and entered the palanquin, which was soon on its way again. She was greeted with a grand celebration in her new home. The relatives were overjoyed to see such a beautiful bride. Madhukar's friends praised his fortune.

When Sadabrij awoke, the parrot gave him the letter. Dejected and disappointed with himself, Sadabrij held the cage and the trident, and briskly started for Dhara Nagar. 'I will find my love, lest I will die,' Sadabrij resolved. He asked Veersen to return to Ambavati and tell his father that Sadabrij had turned spiritual, wandering in search of God. He also told Veersen to tell his father that he would meet them one day.'

Veersen communicated these words to Jagdish. The parents were sad but were happy to know that Sadabrij was alive and would come one day. Enquiring people, Sadabrij reached Saranga's door in the garb of a hermit seeking alms. Saranga, who was eating her meal, recognized Sadabrij's voice. She left her food and got a bowl of rice to give to the hermit. Saranga's mother-in-law objected, suggesting that as a new bride she shouldn't have left her food midway to give alms to a stranger. 'It is sinful for a new bride to keep a saint waiting at the door,' Saranga argued. The old woman was impressed with her daughter-in-law's virtuousness and allowed her to give alms to Sadabrij.

When Sadabrij saw her, he was tempted to embrace her. But Saranga restrained him from acting foolishly. She whispered in his ears and told him to come at night with a dead cobra. 'Come at midnight when everyone is asleep. I will keep the back door open and let you in,' Saranga said.

Sadabrij bought a dead reptile from a snake charmer. As the darkness deepened he snuck into Saranga's room from the back door, a snake in his hands. Saranga was waiting for him. They embraced each other as they had met after a long time. Saranga then separated herself, unveiling her plan, 'I will lie with the snake on my chest, pretending to be dead. After thinking I am dead, the relatives will take me for cremation to the riverbank. You should lurk in the garb of a ghost and get me out of there.'

Sadabrij agreed to the idea. He covered himself with black ash, wore a tiny cloth around his waist and got his hair tangled. Saranga slept with the snake coiled on her chest. As dawn broke and Saranga didn't get up, the women came to check on her. Her sister-in-law first saw the snake on Saranga's chest and got frightened. She began shouting, 'A cobra has bitten Saranga. She is lying dead!'

Others gathered around her and removed the cobra from her chest. They assumed that Saranga was dead as she was not moving at all. A shroud of gloom descended on the relatives. Amidst their wild cries, Brajraj announced, 'What God has willed has happened. We will have to cremate her now.' The relatives took Saranga's body for cremation.

But Sadabrij, who was lurking nearby, emerged, speaking in a scary voice. The people carrying Saranga got terrified and fled. He went to Saranga. She rose and accompanied him to a distant bank of the river. They bathed and refreshed themselves. Then they went to a garden to relax.

While Sadabrij was lying in Saranga's lap, the local king Giland's lustful eyes fell on Saranga. He approached her, pleading, 'I am thirsty. Please give me some water.' Saranga said, 'My husband is lying in my lap. He has my finger between his teeth. I can't fetch water.'

Giland resorted to tricks. He offered Saranga his headgear and asked her to place Sadabrij's head on it. Then he gave her a piece of betel nut, asking her to replace her finger with the nut in Sadabrij's mouth. Fearing that the king might harm her, she rose to fetch water from the nearby well. But Giland dragged her on his horse which galloped to his palace. 'O God! I just got out of a miserable spell. I am in dire straits again!' Saranga sulked.

Giland had several wives. But he was full of lust for Saranga. He offered her all his love if she agreed to marry him.

Saranga acted wisely and said, 'Kindly build a separate palace for me to worship Lord Shiva for some days. After that, I will marry you.' Giland ordered the workers to build a palace for her.

Sadabrij, on the other hand, went to Giland's palace in the garb of a labourer and joined the workers building the palace. Saranga identified Sadabrij and told Giland, 'The labourer is the prince of Ambavati and is my husband.'

Giland who knew Jagdish felt ashamed at what he had done to a neighbouring king's daughter-in-law. He called Sadabrij, gifting him princely attire. He also gave Saranga a bridal dress and begged the couple to forgive him. 'I didn't know that you are the son and daughter-in-law of my venerated friend. Please pardon me,' he said.

Sadabrij politely said, 'You are like my father. Now that I know you picked up Saranga mistakenly, I harbour no ill will against you.' Giland provided them with a chariot which took them home.

Jagdish and Jayanti were excited to see Saranga and Sadabrij. They hosted a lavish party, for which they called Saranga's parents too and happily let Saranga and Sadabrij live as husband and wife. Thereafter, Saranga and Sadabrij lived happily.

If one is determined, one can overcome any hurdle.

Epilogue: How These Tales Were Collected

BIRDS' WISDOM

First things first. 'The Sparrow and Her Crumbs' was the first story I heard when I was very young. It was raining and my aunt, Manorama Devi, was trying to put me to sleep. Both of us lay on a cot in a mud-built room after supper. I was barely six or seven—not old enough to be left alone. Amid the rhythmic fall of raindrops, my aunt whispered the story in my ears. It was delightful. Next morning, when I shared the tale with my father, Anant Sharan Verma, he was quick to ask, 'And what did you learn from the story, my son?'

I said, '*Bahut maja ayeel* (I enjoyed the story a lot).'

'Well, enjoyment is fine. But do you know that the sparrow is one of the smallest and frailest of birds? Yet, she involved the mightiest of entities—the king, his queen, the sea, a snake and an elephant—to get back her morsel of grain,' my father said.

I asked, 'Why did the bird go to the king, queen, sea, snake and elephant to get such a small thing?'

He said, 'A morsel of grain may be a small thing for us. But it meant the world to the bird. It was crucial for her survival. That's why she left no stone unturned to get the grain back. In the quest to achieve her goal, she knocked on the doors of the king, the queen, snake, stick, fire, ocean and the elephant.'

'So, my son,' went on my father, the lesson to be learnt from the story is 'you should never lose heart. You should never give up for your perseverance will surely help you succeed in life. You also learn that even the elephant, though the mightiest of all animals, can be modest enough to listen to the smallest of creatures.'

I had many questions in mind. What happened to the sparrow after she flew off with her crumb? Where did she go? How long did she live?

I asked them in a single breath, but my father did not reply to my questions. 'It is time to get ready for school. Brush your teeth, take a bath and go to school. I will answer all your queries about the sparrow some other time.'

❧

The next day, my father fulfilled his promise when we were resting in our verandah. He began, 'The sparrow was wise and faithful. You have seen how she got her crumb back. Now, see how she saved herself from a cruel crow who was about to eat her up in 'The Crow and the Sparrow' story. You should be wise, faithful and industrious in your life,' my father declared, patting me to sleep. I still remember how I shared enthusiastically the story with my friends in the village and the school.

Over the years, I came to know that this was a famous folk tale that was passed down generation in several parts of Bihar and neighbouring Uttar Pradesh.

❧

THE GREATEST FOLK TALES OF BIHAR

The narrator of the story 'The Village Crow Versus the City Crow' was Gauri Chamar, a farm labourer, who had picked up this story from his workplace somewhere in Punjab.

'A fellow worker from eastern Uttar Pradesh told us this story when we were working in Punjab. We invariably shared this story to counter the urban people when they tried to belittle us,' Gauri would say, after narrating the enchanting tale. Gauri belonged to a sub-section of the Dalit caste, called Chamar, who were mostly engaged in skinning dead cattle and making shoes. Though hailing from a humble background, Gauri had a lot of experience working in faraway cities. He was our window to city life, which we had heard about but never seen, as many of my contemporaries and I were yet to travel beyond our village.

~

'The Stork and Her Husband' was originally a drama often staged in my village in which I had played the role of the male stork in my childhood. Dasrath Lohar would play the banyan tree. Camouflaged in leaves and a trunk, he would pose as a banyan tree. Nandji wore a jute sheet and walked like a four-footed animal in the likeness of a bull. Gayatri, a teenage girl, loved to act as the female stork by donning birds' feathers.

We performed the play in an open field in our village that had no access to any other means of entertainment such as movie theatres or television. Such performances provided the village folk an opportunity to have fun.

I cherish the memory of people clapping when I succeeded in winning over the female stork or performed the act of dying.

The director of the drama was Patru Ahir—an amateur who was primarily a cowherd and farmer. My father, mother and grandmother were in the audience when we performed the drama called 'Baguli baguli kahan jaa-taaru?' (O stork, where are you going?)

The play's tragic end had many in the audience sobbing. I still remember how my grandmother wept watching the last scene of the drama.

~

Phuleshwar Pandey, my first teacher at the village school, had told us the story of 'The Parrot and His Grandson'. As part of his technique to teach with examples, Master Sahib had narrated this story to make us realize how the old parrot taught his grandson the lesson of freedom and how the baby parrot quickly picked it up.

ANIMAL KINGDOM

My father was fond of narrating the saga of 'How a Jackal Attained Pundit-Hood' again and again. While telling it, he would invariably say, 'There is a difference between kindness and foolishness. And there is something known as common sense. The priest acted foolishly when he set a predator free. He lacked common sense too. But the jackal exhibited both wisdom and common sense. The jackal here acted like a real pundit, compelling the priest to pass on the pundit-hood to the clever animal.'

~

It was from 'How the Jackal Preyed on the Goat' that I learnt that jackals were relatively weaker but cleverer than other wild animals. My father had narrated this story to teach me that though unmatched by the physical strength and prowess of lions and tigers, jackals were sharp enough to feed off the kill of the big cats and survive in the wild. 'Brain is mightier than brawn,' my father had told me much before I had experienced the magic of the written word. I loved this story for it helped me reinforce connections with my rural milieu in which goats and jackals were constant fixtures. Our neighbours had goats and we often heard the howls of jackals in the nearby sugar cane and maze fields after sunset.

~

Patru Ahir, a cowherd, would narrate 'The Lioness and the Cow' when we herded our cows together in the fields. Leaving the cows to graze in the fields, we would sit in the shade of a banyan tree near a pond on the outskirts of our village. Patru would tell this story to pass time.

~

Dasrath Lohar had told me 'How the Jackal Got Lessons in Picking Fruits' while we were on our way to a village pond to catch fish. We were going in a group that had many other boys. All of us broke into peals of laughter when we heard it first. Dasrath repeated this story several times on the demand of his peers.

For us it was primarily something entertaining. But Patru, an elderly folklorist, would explain the profound message it carried, 'Getting fruits without putting in efforts is always dangerous. The jackal was hurt because he expected the fruits—either ice apple or mango—without putting in any effort. His sufferings had made him realize the importance of effort. The jackal would wait to see the mangoes falling before his eyes and would eat it then. It meant that the jackal had decided to put in efforts to earn his meal.

~

EPILOGUE : HOW THESE TALES WERE COLLECTED

Basanti Devi, wife of Patru, would tell us the 'Boastful Jackal and Timid Goat' story. Basanti raised goats and cattle in a shed near her house. As a child, I loved it when she told me this story again and again. A next-door neighbour, she always obliged me.

My grandfather one day explain the story to me, 'This is a parable that highlights the value of coexistence. No one should try to impose themselves on others in society. We should maintain harmonious relationship.'

～

Deni Nonia, *who doubled as our domestic help and* washer man, had told us 'The Jackal and the Camel' while escorting us to the pond for a bath. He had narrated several such stories to entertain us. My parents loved Deni for he was a good gossiper and fine entertainer.

～

SURVIVAL IN THE WILD

Patru—the cowherd and folklorist—told me 'The Poor Brahmin and His Seven Daughters'. 'Poverty is the biggest curse. It kills all human emotions. See how poverty led the priest to abandon his daughters in the forest. But fortune plays a great role in life. You never know when and in what way luck will smile on you,' Patru would say in conclusion to the story.

～

My father narrated 'The Fear of Tiptipwa' first. 'The story carried lessons in street-smartness. The old woman acted smartly to fuel confusion in the mind of the tiger and the thief early on. The jackal, too, showed street-smartness against the tiger, averting imminent danger to her family,' my father said. He would ask the children to be street-smart along with gaining knowledge from books.

Sheobachan Ram who ploughed our fields narrated 'The Cobbler and the Washerman.' The story was quite popular among the Dalit castes. The young and the old alike were mesmerized by the story as Sheobachan narrated it, sitting in a farm field or on the edge of the pond in our village.

'Kallu and Mallu used their wisdom to overcome the odds and made fortunes. You should learn lessons in wisdom from Kallu and Mallu,' Sheobachan would say while concluding the story.

❧

FOLK FUN

Phulena Mia, a barber, told me 'The Gossiper' story. He was youthful at that time. He played drums at wedding parties. A quick-witted person, Phulena was quite well known in the village for gossiping. He is old and can't walk around much now. He burst into a hearty laugh when I reminded him of this story during one of my visits to the village. He had to make great efforts to recall the story that he had narrated to us so effortlessly in his youthful days. Phulena told me, '*Babu, jamana badal gael ba. Bahot sara kahani hamahin bhula gaeel baani. Ab koi sun-e wala naikh-e* (Son, times have changed. I have myself forgotten many of the stories. There is no one to listen to such stories now).'

❧

Ramchandra Kurmi—a cowherd and cultivator had narrated 'The Simpleton'. Ramchandra would narrate it to pull the Bitandi's leg who, though a blacksmith by caste, did not know how to make sickles and spades. Bitandi was a simpleton who was unable to learn the skill a blacksmith was supposed to. Though narrated to make fun of Bitandi, it was not invented by Ramchandra. He had learnt it from his elders in the village. Bitandi had fretted and fumed while Ramchandra had told the story. The other villagers, however, had enjoyed it a lot, laughing their hearts out.

~

Mangla Lal—a resident of my village—had narrated 'Munshiji and Raiji'. An old man coming from the Kayestha caste of pen-pushers, Mangla Lal had worked as a munshi during the British rule, collecting taxes and surveying land. Though the British era had become part of history long ago, Mangla Lal loved telling this story to prove the supremacy of pen—a symbol of wisdom—over baton that symbolized brute power.

His clout had waned as the rules of *malguzari* collection had eased and the district collectors in Independent India were not as harsh on the cultivators as their peers in British India used to be. He rued the demise of the Raj and was never tired of extolling the British rulers' firm enforcement of rules. The youths teased and poked fun at him for his patronizing words for the erstwhile colonial masters but enjoyed his stories.

GODS, DEMONS AND FAITH

My grandfather, Panchdeo Narayan Lal, had narrated to me the story of 'The Priest and the Thugs'. Grandpa was a religious person with strong faith in God. He used to say that God appreciated devotion. 'If you are a true devotee, you can get to see Him,' Grandpa would assert, citing this story as an example.

I enjoyed listening to the priest's funny acts always landing the thieves in trouble. As a young boy, I loved the character of the priest more than that of the thieves. Still, I was unable to convince myself that God had appeared physically to save the priest when he was going to die.

But Grandpa wanted me to believe in God. He felt that if I had unwavering faith in God, I would do well in life. So, he told me another story to convince me how God listened to true believers and physically appeared before them.

❧

'Now, you must believe in the existence of God. Hanumanji loves children. If you recite the Hanuman Chalisa, a devotional poem in praise of Lord Hanuman, before going to write your examinations, you will never fail. You should memorize the Hanuman Chalisa and recite it every day,' my grandfather instructed while concluding the 'The Young Boy and Hanumanji' story. I might have been about ten to twelve year old then. I don't know if I developed faith in Hanumanji, but I memorized Hanuman Chalisa nonetheless and recited it every day before going to school hoping to succeed in exams.

❧

Gajadhar Mishra was our *purohit*. I had heard him telling the 'The Skull and Raghobaba' story many times. While narrating the story, he would quote several shlokas from Sanskrit scriptures to explain the philosophy of karma and destiny. I have not quoted the Sanskrit couplets but retained the essence of the story, which I enjoyed listening to in my formative years. Later, I came to know that it was an old folk story known

EPILOGUE: HOW THESE TALES WERE COLLECTED

to many people, particularly those who performed religious rituals for others.

~

Harishankar Mishra, Gajadhar Mishra's younger brother, would tell us the story of 'The Rakshasi's Sacrifice'. 'Some demons are more virtuous than human beings. See, how the rakshasi had better human qualities and how the prince was devoid of any sense of gratitude,' the priest would point out while concluding the story.

~

Maunia Baba, a sanyasi, had narrated 'The Elephant and the Worms' story. Maunia Baba lives in an orchard on the outskirts of Chakri village, three kilometres west of my village. In his seventies now, he observed *maun vrat* for twelve long years. Most of the time loitering around in silence, he would talk by moving only his hands, arms or head.

I had first seen him in the 1970s during his silent wanderings when he would occasionally drop by at our home. After observing silence for twelve years, Maunia Baba dug a tunnel and began living inside it. For the next twelve years, the tunnel became his home, away from sunlight and the public glare. It was said that Baba would come out of his resting place at midnight to meet his mother who fed him fruits and milk.

After spending another twelve long years in the tunnel, he came out and performed a *yajna* in the same orchard. Thereafter, he ended his self-imposed silence and resumed speaking, drawing lots of people for his darshan. Now, Maunia Baba is busy building a grand temple with the donation from his devotees.

What differentiates Maunia Baba from modern-day TV

gurus and Babas is his dislike for publicity and the media glare. He also shuns politics. If he talks at all, it's mostly about the philosophy of karma, and the secrets of life and death besides the Gods and Goddesses. While narrating this story, he emphasized, 'Every creature reaps what it sows, and unchangeable reality of life is that we have to die once we are born. A saint or a common man—we have to suffer the consequences of our wrong actions. So, always try to lead a pious and virtuous life. There are 84 lakh yonis (breeds) in this mortal world. We have to transit through all these breeds in the course of the cycle of deaths and rebirths,' Maunia Baba told me, citing the example of the fisherman born as the elephant.

❦

Sughar Ram, a village elder from Chamar caste, was the first to have told me 'The Brahmin and the Washerwoman' story. Sughar was an accomplished folklorist who sang and danced to the tune of *pakhauj* on the occasion of Holi. Sughar is no more now. His grandson, Satyendra Ram, is a village-level social activist. Sughar had narrated this story to emphasize how life was subservient to destiny. Satyendra looked much amused when I told him how his grandfather had narrated this story to me. He enjoyed it too. Sughar had died much before Satyendra was perceptive enough to understand his grandfather's tales. He wished to preserve the stories his grandfather was loved for by his fellow villagers.

PRANKS, INTRIGUES, STRUGGLE AND ENTERTAINMENT

Basudeo Lal, a farmer and popular folklorist, had narrated the story of 'The Scholar and His Heavenly Beard'. I had first heard it at a village chowpal, where people had gathered around a bonfire on a wintery night during my childhood. Basudeo had many such stories to narrate, causing the listeners to burst into peals of laughter. He was a much-sought-after storyteller invited by residents of many other villages in the area to be entertained by his tales in verse. He was very good at singing ballads as well.

I had heard the 'Malpua Tale' from Saral Dusadh, a landless labourer. This story sought to emphasize that poverty could breed pettiness. 'Extreme poverty can turn even a loving relationship between husband and wife sour,' Saral would say while narrating this story. Saral was a Dusadh—a sub-caste among Dalits which lived on rearing pigs. Saral would also sing folk songs with themes on poverty and deprivation.

I first heard the 'Andheri Nagari, Chowpat Raja' from my Sanskrit teacher, Vaidyanath Mishra, when I was in Class VIII student at Dronacharya High School at Done, four kilometres from my village. Master Sahib, as we called him, knew many such stories. He loved telling us stories that were not part of the syllabus. We eagerly waited for his classes to listen to such stories. He was, probably, the first to acquaint us with *Panchatantra*—an ancient series of folk-tales.

But 'Andher Nagri Chaupat Raja' (the original title of this story) is not part of the *Panchtantra* series. We were quite fond of this story and would often request him to tell it. Master Sahib was only too eager to oblige us.

'If foolish and whimsical, you are doomed like the stupid king,' Master Sahib would enlighten us while concluding the story. Later, I discovered that 'Andher Nagri Chaupat Raja' was also a popular adage used by people in the countryside to describe bizarre acts of stupidity by someone in the position of authority.

～

My mother, Manorama Devi (a namesake of my aunt) who had told me 'The Sparrow and Her Crumb' story also shared the story of 'The Sinner and the Khaini' to instil a sense of morality in me after she got scent of my crush on a fifteen-year-old neighbourhood girl. She was a lone student in my class. I would steal a look at her every few minutes in the classroom and would let go of no opportunity to hang around her.

With my infatuation growing by the day, I began to lose interest in my studies. Every day, I waited for her to come out to pluck leaves of green mustard and peas cooked as saag.

Sensing my interest in her, she, too, started responding to my advances. A tall girl of fair complexion, she was almost my age. I liked everything about her—her bewitching smile and full lips, and her long black hair snaking down to her slender waist—assets that made her a real looker, a treat for the eyes. The urge to touch her would drive me insane.

One day, I saw my lady love enter a field to pluck peas and mustard leaves like always. Sensing an opportunity, I threw a hurried glance around to make sure there were no prying eyes watching. Satisfied, I tiptoed to where my fair one was standing—amidst a thick growth of mustard plants with their yellow flowers in full bloom, providing a romantic background. As I approached my 'sweetheart', she turned around and cast a look at me that suggested she didn't disapprove of my intrusion. I dropped all inhibitions to ask her for a kiss. A 'willing partner', she hinted agreement. We reclined in a tight embrace with our

EPILOGUE : HOW THESE TALES WERE COLLECTED

lips locked, and our two hearts beating each to each.

But as ill luck would have it, her father suddenly appeared from nowhere and caught us in the act. Lest the episode was publicized, damaging the family's reputation, her father said and did nothing at that time. But he dragged his daughter home and beat her up mercilessly. After punishing her, he came to my house and complained to my mother about my 'mischief'.

The wise woman that she was, my mother neither scolded me nor gave a thrashing. Instead, she just told me this story after the girl's father left to halt my deviation from the path of 'correctness.'

Although I was not accused of something that the character in the story had done (of raping the destitute woman), my mother—like most of the parents of her generation—treated romantic dalliance of underage boys and girls as act of moral turpitude and hence forbidden.

My mother is alive. She now treats me as a paragon of virtue. I, too, love her and feel indebted to her for raising me in a decent manner and telling me wonderful stories during my childhood that helped shape my character in my early days.

❦

My childhood friend, Bhrigunath Sharma, had first told me the 'The Leaf and the Lump' story. He had narrated it when we were in Class IX at the Dronacharya High school, Done, three kilometres from our village. We would walk through thorny stretches of farm fields and woods for about forty-five minutes to reach our school. At times, we had to brave rain and storms on the way along with scorching heat in summer and bone-chilling cold in the winter.

Bhrigunath and I were inseparable friends. His house was

about 300 metres away from mine in the village. But we always lived together—either I would go to the Bhrigunath's hut or he would come to my mud house. My mother loved Bhrigunath and Bhrigu's mother fawned upon me. Bhrigunath and I were good students too. We were among the five of the 100 students in our class who had cleared the matriculation examination conducted by the Bihar School Examination Board. The rest had failed.

Unlike the lump and leaf, we got separated once we finished schooling. I went to Gaya—a faraway city of international repute, where Gautam Buddha attained enlightenment centuries ago— in pursuit of higher education. Bhrigunath got enrolled in a district-level college at Siwan, about 30 kilometres from our village. We may have been separated to pursue a career, but our friendship has survived the rough and tumble of life to this day. Bhrigu and I always looked forward to spending time together after coming home for holidays. We felt happy in each other's company more than anyone else's.

We still spend most of the time together whenever I happen to visit my village, often recounting this story and laughing.

∽

Baleshwar Mistri, a blacksmith, had narrated the 'Ulua, Bulua and I' story. Baleshwar's son, Dasrath, was my friend.

∽

Dulai Mia—our family hairdresser—would tell me the 'Badshah and His Youngest Daughter' story while trapping my head between his knees so that I could not shake my head while he was cropping my hair.

∽

EPILOGUE: HOW THESE TALES WERE COLLECTED

Our teacher Vaidyanath Mishra had narrated 'The Shyamkaran Horse' story in the classroom.

~

'The Mahout and the Dogs' story is basically an explanation of a popular adage: 'One can't dodge bad times.' Ravidra Tiwary, our driver, narrated it to me.

~

My grandfather first narrated the 'Bharbitan' story to me, conveying the message that a dwarf, too, can turn his fortune around through hard work, a positive attitude and grace of God.

BHIKHARI THAKUR'S POPULAR FOLKLORES

'Gabarghichor', 'Beti Viyog' and 'Vidhwa Vilap' are the plays authored, enacted and staged by Bhikhari Thakur (1887—1971), the greatest folklorist of the Bhojpuri dialect. I had watched Bhikhari Thakur's band members playing 'Gabarghchore', 'Beti Viyog' and 'Vidhwa Vilap'. I have paraphrased 'The Daughter's Suffering' by clubbing the two plays—'Beti Viyog' and 'Vidhwa Vilap'—without interfering with the essence and message of the two great plays of the time.

'Saranga and Sadabrij' is an oral novel filled with ballads. Its original author is not known. But it has been on the villagers' lips for generations. I had heard it first when Patru Ahir had narrated it in my village streets in 1970s. Only a good singer could have narrated the love story of Saranga and Sadabrij, who conversed in verses through their twelve lives full of struggle and intrigues.

Acknowledgements

This book is dedicated to my mother, Manorama Devi.

I am indebted to my parents, grandparents and the villagers who raised me in the midst of these fantastic stories. Some of them are alive and some have moved to heaven. This book is a result of their collaborative efforts, love, good wishes and blessings.

I am hugely indebted to my living god, Ramanuj 'Bhaiya', who showed me the path to the world of Gods, Goddesses, ghosts, demons, myths and realities, and has been kind to me all my life.

Huge thanks to my literary agent, Suhail Mathur—the first reader of my book—and his team members at Book Bakers.

Special thanks to Lalu Prasad Yadav for explaining the stories of Bhikhari Thakur to me, and the Rupa team for working so hard on the manuscript.

Tons of thanks to my role model in journalism and writing, A.J. Philip, and my friends, Dinesh Kumar Singh, Gupteshwar Pandey, R. Rajagopal, Devdan Mitra, Mammen Matthew, Prem Kumar Mani, Anurag Anand, Shakeel Ahmad, Sumit Bhattacharya, Venkitesh Ramakrishnan, Krishna Kumar

Dvivedi and Raj Kumar for their feedback and valuable additions.

So long is the list of contributors that I can't possibly name everyone. The ones I do remember to thank are, alphabetically, all Ajays and Ashoks I know, Amit, Anand, Devraj, Faizan, Fariyal, Dipak, Piyush, Kanhaiya, R.K. Sinha (MP), Manish, Prakash, Ramashankar, Roshan, all Sanjays I know, Sanjeev, Shambhavi, Suchishmita, Surendraji, Sumi and Shrikant.

Thanks to my daughters, Sonali and Saloni, who read and added value to the stories and who are better storytellers than I am.

My wife, Manju—my life support.

Loved younger ones, Raju, Tunna, Kunkun, Pratima, Kumud Kiran, Swati, Sunny, Vicky, Manni, Neha, Prabhat, Binny, Saket, Noopur, Nikki, Nidhi, Chhotu, Rishu, Jhisi, Aditya and Akshata.

Last but not the least, all the sparrows, crows, parrots, jackals, dogs, donkeys and horses I lived, played and grew up with in my village.

Thank you, Bihar, my home state and its people—for everything.

Glossary

Mahiya	a local sweet
Kaluhari	where sugarcane is juiced
Mitha	jaggery
Chacha	uncle
Kadahi	a huge frying pan
Bhatthi	furnace
Jhal, Majira, Pakwaj	local musical instruments
Hawaijahaj	airplane
Chowpal	assembly of people
Ghulami	slavery
Basant	spring
Devar	husband's younger brother
Bhabhi	wife of elder brother
Chaita	a kind of folk song
Kaud	bonfire
Pagdandi	pathway
Bahelia	bird catcher
Kalyug	the age of downfall
Raiyat	peasant
Chamar	a caste

Malpua	a delicacy made of sugar, ghee and flour
Biraha	a kind of folk song
Khadau	wooden slippers
Dhoban	a woman belonging to a low untouchable caste that earns a living washing other's clothes
Malik	master
Khaini	raw tobacco
Gulli-danda	a local game played with a stick and wooden ball
Haal	hockey
Luka-chhipi	hide-and-seek
Garai	a kind of fish
Badshah	a Muslim king
Harunipankha	hand-operated fan
Thela	cart
Panch	village arbitrator
Joran	curd culture
Virya	sperm
Hajam	barber
Baratis	groom's relatives and friends
Beti bechwa	one who sells his/her daughter
Vidai	farewell
Kaki	aunt
Pavitrata	purity
Pari	fairy
Sohar	a type of song that is sung to mark the joyous occasion of childbirth in a family
Sindurdan	a ritual in which the groom applies vermilion on the bride's forehead to

	consummate the marriage
Malguzari	land taxes
Purohit	family priest
Maun vrat	the practice of observing silence
Yagya	yajna, saintly ritual
Pakhauj	a local musical instrument